MW01168817

THE WEDDING PROMISE

The Bridesmaid Series | Book 1

MELINDA CURTIS

THE WEDDING PROMISE
The Bridesmaid Series Book 1
Melinda Curtis

©Melinda Curtis 2014

❀ Created with Vellum

CHAPTER 1

IT WAS RAINING. Again.

Tiffany Bonander tried humming a few bars of White Christmas. It was, after all, December 23. Cheer was called for.

But the incessant beat of fat raindrops on the tangled foliage of the Ecuadorian rainforest and on her pink rain slicker, drowned out her cheer.

Or maybe she was just drowning under the pressure of heavy responsibilities.

Ankle-deep water rushed down the steep, muddy road toward Tiff and her precious cargo—thirty pounds of cocoa beans. She couldn't lose the beans. They were the answer to all her troubles.

Thunder boomed. And boomed again. The downpour increased to a deluge.

Tightening her grip on the wheelbarrow handles, Tiff tried to find purchase with her rain boots, tried to make it to the next rise before the road turned into a river. Tried...and failed. Somewhere above her the river had risen high enough to crest a bank. Water surged toward her.

Tiff's father claimed they'd abandoned this cocoa plantation years ago for drainage reasons. He should have used the F-word: *flood.*

Tiff stumbled to her knees, and water rushed into her boots—cute, pink-flowered plastic ones which quickly filled with water and felt as heavy as cement shoes. If not for her grip on the wheelbarrow, she might have been swept downhill. Just last week, she'd heard about a woman who'd been carried away by the cresting river and smashed into a tree. Smashed as in: *to pieces. Dead.*

That would be worse than being broke and the laughing-stock of the civilized world.

This was karma, plain and simple. She shouldn't have jilted Chad at their engagement party or left Malcolm at the altar.

Get a grip, Tiff.

Her father's angry voice crested above the approaching thunder. *"You have an idea to save this company? You've had five fiancés in four years, Tiffany—and no marriages! No one takes you seriously, including me. Get a grip."*

She'd like to get a handle on things. A do-over for starters. She would've avoided New York's social circus and gossip columns, would've been more careful about how she qualified love, and been less trusting that her father could successfully run their family's chocolate business. If Daddy had made a few more sound management decisions and squandered less money, she wouldn't have had to come to Ecuador at all.

A primal sound escaped Tiff's throat. Had she been in New York, she'd have been mortified. But here? In the remote Ecuadorian wilderness? No one was around to see the Bon-Bon Heiress have a meltdown.

Tiff levered herself to her feet, feeling more like Frankenstein plodding along in her water-filled boots than Christopher Robin skipping on a blustery day.

She inched her wheelbarrow through the sludgefest only to slip into a rut. Her foot came out of her water-logged boot, and the flood water carried it away. The wind whipped off her hood.

Rain plastered her hair to her head, and ran down her back. The right handle of the wheelbarrow broke.

Helpless. Bootless. Prince Charming-less.

Tiff would not cry. She hefted the bag of cocoa beans to her shoulders. Her machete swung at her hip as if she was a big, bad jungle babe. *As if...*

The water continued to rise, funneling down the road, rising above her ankles.

I hate the rain. I hate the rainforest. I hate the jungle.

It wouldn't be as wet and muddy beneath the treeline. But that was where everything in the vicinity would be seeking shelter. Everything she feared–leopards, spiders, snakes. Anything could be in there. Anything.

I miss high heels, designer clothes, and a healthy bank balance.

A rat washed toward her, scrambling to find purchase on her remaining boot. Tiff shrieked and lumbered for the rainforest, pushing her way through the heavy undergrowth like the token stupid girl in a horror movie. The one destined to die first.

Don't panic. Don't panic.

A branch hit her in the face. Tiff stopped. Reminded herself to breathe. Tried not to think about leopards and spiders and snakes. She tugged her machete free and swung it without finesse, hacking a path through shoots, vines, and broad leaves.

She tried not to recall jungle-set movies where *things* erupted from the shadows and *killed* the unsuspecting.

Too late.

Hack-step. *Jurassic Park*. Hack-step. *Predator*. Hack-step. *Anaconda*.

She watched too many movies. But she was an aberration of her generation. She hated anything with zombies. They gave her the heebie-jeebies. And B-flicks with spiders and snakes...

Don't think about spiders.

Hack-step. Hack-step.

Don't think about snakes.

Snakes dangled from trees. Snakes lurked in bushes. Snakes ruled the foliage.

The sky darkened and rumbled. Everything around her became murky and shadowed.

Think happy thoughts.

Rainbows, and dandelions, and sales at Nieman's.

A series of lightning strikes was followed immediately by earth-shaking booms.

Hack-step.

Something large startled behind the bush she'd chopped.

She screamed.

The large something stumbled forward. Man-size and zombie-like.

Her scream turned into a wail of terror. She backpedaled into a tree trunk, hitting it with a solid thunk that made the world look bright and sparkly, like Times Square on New Year's Eve. She slung the bag of beans forward into the mud, hoping the zombie would trip over it.

Something tumbled in the branches above her. And plunged. And plummeted. And landed on the other side of the tree.

Simultaneously, the large something that had startled her originally stumbled within striking distance.

The world became less sparkly. Tiff held up her machete like a light saber. "Stay back!"

The rain seemed to let up.

Hands reached toward her.

The fallen something behind her hissed.

Zombie or snake? Zombie or—

Another hiss.

Tiff leapt forward into the arms of zombie-man.

SOMEONE WAS SCREAMING.

Jackson Hardaway hoped to hell it wasn't him.

He knew he was in a rainforest. It smelled like the underside of his grandmother's refrigerator—moist, dank, and decaying. He'd veered off the road when the rain stopped misting and got serious, immediately regretting not buying a machete when he'd started his trek a week ago.

As soon as he was under the trees, the gathering storm had unleashed thunder and lightning, triggering his anxiety about the war—about Owen, about blood and fear—until visions of bomb blasts and men's screams filled his head.

Didn't matter that he knew he was in Ecuador in the midst of a downpour. Made no difference that he knew thunder wasn't a bomb blast and lightning wasn't the resulting explosion. Jax saw again flashes of light filling the desert night sky like the finale in a Fourth of July parade. The roar. The despair. The screaming.

"Don't die." He tried to staunch the blood pumping from Owen's chest, heedless of the blood spurting from a wound below his own knee.

Someone slammed into him. The screaming grew louder.

Still in the throes of memory, Jax assumed Owen smacked into him—wounded, panicked, screaming. Maybe in this reality, Jax could save his comrade. He pressed his hands against Owen's chest.

"What are you doing? *Don't!*" A woman's voice. A sweet, flowery scent. A pair of small, yet determined hands shoving his off her chest.

Oops.

The vestiges of Afghanistan faded, turning his vision into a black screen. So not helpful. Jax flinched at another rocket blast/roll of thunder.

"Snake! Snake! Snake!" The woman scuttled behind him. Her fingers dug into his rain-slickered shoulder near the strap of his backpack.

Jax willed his vision to clear.

"It's coming. And it looks hungry." Her hysteria was a hot, tangible thing, frosted with a slight New York accent. It made him hot and cold at the same time.

"Maybe you should run." How he wished he could follow her. But running blind through the jungle was the quickest way to get himself killed.

She tugged him back a step. "*We* should run. Come on."

A splinter of light pierced his vision. "Come on, come on, come on," he murmured. Snake. Jungle. Nice smelling damsel in distress. It'd be great to see about now.

"That's what I said. Come on." She tugged him back another step.

That step being taken with his bionic leg, he nearly fell and became snake bait.

She tugged on his straps and saved him from falling. "Here. If you won't run, take my machete and kill it." She was a blood-thirsty New Yorker. Sure, she lacked the common sense to retreat, but she got points for keeping him alive. She pressed a leather grip into his right palm. "Off with its humongous head!"

Humongous?

The grip was sturdy, giving him something to hold onto. The splinter of light became several. His vision kaleidoscoped.

Be in the here and now, buddy. Blink-blink-blink.

"Where's the snake?" he asked. Was it too much to hope for that the city girl was having a freak-out over a fallen branch?

It was. He sensed movement at his feet. *Screw this.* His machete-free hand reached behind him.

"*Seriously?* Are you blind? It's right there—three feet from your boot!" She capped off this news flash with a loud noise that was half-scream, half-amateur opera note.

Her panic pierced the fog in his brain. His vision came back with dizzying intensity. He snapped his weapon free of its holster as the snake came into nightmarish focus. It was big enough to eat a pre-teen, and slithering toward his real foot!

Jax's shot echoed through the rainforest.

"You missed." The woman released him, taking the scent of civilization with her. "You shot my cocoa beans."

"I wasn't aiming at the snake." He'd done enough killing to last a few lifetimes. "I wanted to scare it off."

The snake changed direction and moved fast into the shadowy underbrush.

"That's it. The cap to my perfect day. Saved by a gun-toting tree-hugger." She elbowed Jax aside, walking too close to the bush the snake had disappeared under with a lopsided gait he was all too familiar with. Only she walked funny because her footwear didn't match—one flower-booted foot, one muddy-socked foot.

She was a wisp of a woman. Barely over five feet. Soaking wet, like she was now, she'd be lucky to weigh in at a hundred pounds. Dark brown hair was plastered to her head. The hood of her pink rain slicker was off. The continuous downpour made it too murky to make out much about her face, except it was scrunched in disapproval. She knelt near a shredded bag, right next to Mr. Snake's bush.

He holstered his weapon, and hauled her back a few feet.

"Hey." She tried shrugging out of his grip.

"Snake Bait." The nickname fit. "Best we leave the area before that reptile changes his mind." Jax kept an eye on the foliage.

"I need those beans, Tree-Hugger." The snap in her voice gave the impression she'd be willing to wrestle that snake for possession if it dared show up again.

"Don't tell me." He kept an eye on the underbrush. "Those are magic beans."

She tried to loosen his fingers on her collar. When that didn't work, she struck his right in-step with her booted foot.

He didn't so much as flinch.

"*Ow.*" She hunched over. "What kind of boot is that?"

"It's no boot." He released her. "It's my prosthesis."

CHAPTER 2

HE SAID THE WORD, "*PROSTHESIS*," like Tiff said the word, "*Snake*."

"I'm sorry." Tiff grimaced at the pain in her foot and ankle, and the guilt caused by her embarrassing social blunder. "You're American and probably fought for my freedom, right?" He nodded. "Then you saved me, and here I am, acting ungrateful."

Something snapped in the direction the snake had disappeared into. She jumped back.

Her rescuer was tall enough to hide behind, with strong, almost gaunt features, and the bluest eyes she'd ever seen. "I don't wear a sign that says my leg's missing from the knee down. I'm flattered you couldn't tell I'm a..."

That awkward pause. He could have filled it with harsh words–like cripple or invalid or something equally self-deprecating. Her heart went out to him.

"That you're a *veteran*," she finished for him. Actually, her first thought when she'd caught sight of him had been less charitable. He'd been stumbling forward in camouflage clothing with his eyes closed. She'd thought the zombie apocalypse had begun.

But now wasn't the time for fantasies, creepy or otherwise (the otherwise being based on intense blue eyes and heroic rescues). "I'd love to stay and chat, but I need to get my beans to a dry place and then backtrack for my wheelbarrow."

Something screeched, a spine-tingling sound with a strangled finish.

I hate the jungle.

Tiff realized she was gripping his pack straps once more. She released him. "On second thought, I'll leave the wheelbarrow rescue for another day."

"What about your boot?" Her rescuer's grin was lopsided, as if he didn't trust himself to go crazy and get caught smiling. Might ruin that intensely serious vibe he presented.

"My boot is probably at the bottom of the valley by now." If not on its way to being washed into the lower fork of the river and eventually out to sea.

He handed her the machete. "You should have boots that lace up, not slip on." He said it kindly when he could just as easily have made her feel foolish for her rubber, flowery boots.

As if it hadn't already ruined her day, the rain came down harder.

Heeding his advice about the snake, she crouched as far away from the undergrowth as she could and still reach her gun-shot cocoa beans. She gathered up the frayed ends of burlap and black plastic, and slung what was left of the bag over her shoulder. It was depressingly lighter than it had been before. Hopefully, she had enough to convince her father the quality of the beans here were worth investing in. Rejuvenating the family's cocoa fields with a new strain of cocoa would save the family chocolate business.

"Well," she tried to sound cheerful. As cheerful as one could sound with one boot lost and half her experiment destroyed. "I need to get across the bridge." Or she'd be stuck on this side of the river with a big, hungry snake, and a handsome, wounded warrior. Both of which were dangerous in their own way.

"I'm headed the other way." He reached beneath his rain

slicker to adjust his backpack straps. "Been nice bumping into you, Snake Bait."

Tiff caught his arm. "Downhill?" Through her family's cocoa fields and up the other side of the valley?

He nodded.

"Uhm. The buildings down there were washed away years ago." She rested her socked-foot on her boot. "The river's cresting. If anyone's going to be snake bait, it'll be you. Where are you headed? Is it close? Is there shelter?"

"I'm going to Quito."

She must have heard him wrong. "Quito is three hundred miles from here."

His blue eyes turned as stormy as the sky above them.

"I know it's none of my business, but do you realize the nearest village in the direction you're going is thirty miles away? And the track past my family's cocoa fields is more like a goat trail?" They were the last lowland valley before the Andes range officially began soaring to the heavens.

"I know where I'm going," he said with all the cockiness of a man unwilling to ask directions when he was clearly lost. "Besides, there's nothing the way you're going either. Not for miles."

"There's the bus stop and the convent where the road widens on the other side of the river." The convent being her grandparents' former plantation home, currently presided over by three elderly nuns.

Their original convent had collapsed in an earthquake several years ago and Tiff's father had given them the property. Four days a week, the elderly nuns took the bus to the nearest village where they taught locals how to read, provided rudimentary medical care, and held religious services in a clearing behind the small grocery. Living with the nuns was like living with three Jewish grandmothers–they bestowed upon Tiff equal parts love and criticism.

"I need to be going." He must have moved into a shaft of

light or perhaps the clouds above broke. In either case, she noticed blood on his pants leg.

"Hey, you're bleeding!"

In typical military fashion, he did a full-body check when he most likely knew the blood was coming from the vicinity of his knee.

"Predators smell blood," she said. Jaguars. Panthers. And maybe snakes?

"It'll wash out in the rain." So confident.

He pushed her buttons. "If you don't bleed to death first."

More intense blue-eyed defiance. "It's oozing. I didn't slice an artery."

"But–"

"Snake Bait, it's been fun. But I need to make my miles for the day." In two steps, he was swallowed by the jungle.

Okay, then. "Merry Christmas, Tree-Hugger." Tiff headed uphill, hacking a path with her machete. But worry for her rescuer lingered. He hadn't been able to see the snake. Was he sick? Seriously injured? Feverish?

The roar of the river drowned out the barrage of rain and her concern for anyone other than herself. The bridge spanning its banks was a combination of rusted steel and rotted wood. It would have been condemned had it existed in the states. The water had risen significantly since the morning and was now within two feet of the bridge deck. Further down, it spilled over the lower bank and curled onto the track downhill.

Tiff had never visited Ecuador during the rainy season. In the plantation's hey-day, she and her brother had ridden her grandfather's four-wheeler to-and-from the cocoa fields to the main house above the river. Back then, she'd had no fear of the jungle, no fear of a flood. As children, they'd never been left on their own. Their days were spent in the fields under the careful supervision of her grandfather. Their nights were spent listening to stories about starting the business and cultivating the land. Tiff could still hear her grandfather's voice as he spoke of the rich quality of Arriba chocolate, of the care needed to graft and cross-pollinate the cocoa trees for a richer, healthier crop.

Years later, Tiff's dad wasn't buying any Arriba cocoa beans, their fields were in danger of being swallowed up by the jungle, and Bon-Bon Chocolate had been called out by competitors for skimping on quality. Her father and brother were focused on maximizing profits, draining the company dry. Tiff wanted the company to go on. She wanted something to pass on to her children. She'd come to Ecuador, cleared a small plot around the healthiest cocoa trees, and grafted different varieties to the family's original stock. The cocoa beans she carried were the first fruits of her labor. All she needed to do was dry them out and test their quality.

Tiff kept one hand on the rickety railing the entire way across the bridge, only slipping once, sending her socked-foot plunging into the roaring river. Her heart had plunged along with it. A few pulse-slowing minutes later, she reached the collapsed lean-to that served as the bus stop. Tiff picked her way carefully over a narrow pebbled path behind it to the convent. Thankfully, she arrived without stepping on anything jagged or mushy or alive.

The convent was built on stilts. Upstairs, the common area was a kitchen and dining room, and was smaller than most studio apartments in New York. Off the common area were four small bedrooms, one bathroom, and a storage room. Tiff's drying racks were underneath the house. She went there first, on the lookout for predatory wildlife–*big or small*–that might have sought shelter from the rain. Finding none, she emptied her bag onto the rack, and spread the cocoa beans over the mesh. She sent up a silent prayer that they'd dry properly. With the soaking they'd had and the humidity in the air, it seemed more likely they'd mold. Or taste like gun powder.

Tiff entered the convent through the cock-eyed front door, the wood having rotted through beneath the bottom hinge on the doorframe. She shed her boot and muddied sock, hung up her rain slicker, and placed her empty, dripping bag on a hook. Then she donned a pair of pink flip-flops. With all the wildlife in Ecuador, no one ever went barefoot, even inside.

Sister Mary Ofelia sat on a wobbly bench at the kitchen table, giving a garlic clove a good pressing and giving Tiff an assessing once-over. Her black habit hung askew from her thin frame, like an ill-fitting hospital gown. "*You've lost a pretty boot,*" she said in Spanish.

"*Another tragedy.*" Another urgent trip to the large market three villages away. Tiff washed up in the sink.

After Tiff changed into dry clothes, she joined Sister Mary Ofelia at the table to help cut vegetables for dinner. Meals in this part of Ecuador were mostly vegetable-based with a side of rice.

"*One boot.*" Sister Mary Ofelia tilted her head. "*Pray to Saint Anthony and it will show up.*"

There was a higher likelihood of Prince Charming appearing with a glass slipper and a marriage proposal. That boot was halfway to the Galapagos by now.

Hunched over her cane, Sister Mary Lucia did a slow shuffle into the room toward the table. Reddish-brown freckles blanketed her features and disappeared into her wrinkles. Sister Mary Rosa trailed after her, wheeling a walker over the creaky wood floor. She was a spritely thing, about Tiff's size, with a gap-toothed smile that was contagious.

Sister Mary Rosa detoured from the table to the remains of Tiff's bag by the door. She fingered the shredded burlap and sniffed. "*Gunshot?*"

Three pairs of eyes turned to Tiff with curiosity.

"*There was a stranger and a snake on the road.*" It sounded as if Tiff was telling a bad joke. *A man with one leg bumps into a woman and a snake during a rainstorm.* All she needed was the addition of three nuns and a punch line. *Ba-dum-bum.*

Silence descended, with a backdrop of steady rain on the tin roof. The nuns weren't conversationalists. They were put on the earth to spread the gospel, not gossip.

"*You brought the wheelbarrow back?*" Sister Mary Ofelia asked.

Tiff suppressed a groan. "*It's at the bottom of the hill.*" She hoped.

The nuns sighed in unison, as if they knew they'd never see their wheelbarrow again, as if they knew Tiff had no idea what she was doing alone, in Ecuador, on an abandoned cocoa plantation.

She was afraid they were right.

JAX SLID in the mud on his backside.

A long way this time.

Down the hill and into a bush at the bend in the road.

At least it's the direction I'm headed.

He had trouble getting traction with his prosthetic. Even if he'd had spiked cleats on both feet, he'd probably still slip-and-slide down the hill on his butt. He'd chosen this route for its directness to Quito. It might have been smarter to keep to the well-traveled roads.

His leg hurt. His prosthetic wasn't sealing on the short spur of bone beneath his knee. He'd tried to adjust it after he'd left Snake Bait, but he needed to dry everything off. The layers of sock and polyurethane were supposed to be lubed, not wet. Certainly not wet with blood from skin rubbed raw.

This wasn't how he envisioned his trek for a fallen comrade. The rain wasn't the issue. It was the mud and the way the road had turned into a river. And how he felt hungry and weak and pitiful. Like a cripple.

Familiar resentment roiled in his gut, boiled over through his limbs. *A cripple?* He rejected the label.

Jax scrambled to his feet. Wet. Muddy. In pain. But not helpless. Never—

The mud beneath his prosthetic gave way and he clutched at the bush. Something popped free from its lower branches—a pink, flowery rubber boot.

Jax grabbed it before it was carried away by the rushing water.

Snake Bait.

Thinking about their encounter made him smile. She'd mentioned a bus stop and a convent on the other side of the river. Up the hill. Subtracting precious mileage from his trip odometer.

Up the hill was a roof over his head and a woman who smelled of wildflowers, talked a tough game, and was missing a pink boot.

His goal was the opposite direction. More than three hundred miles. And it didn't look like there was any shelter ahead.

Not that being with Mother Nature bothered him. As a kid, he'd roughed it on overnight hikes. As a soldier, he'd bedded down in a lot of hell-holes. But this was different. Until he reached flat ground, it'd be like sleeping in a river, no telling what washed down his way. Tree branches, rubber boots, snakes. He had to move on. But it was becoming increasingly apparent to him that Snake Bait might have been right. The safest place to wait out the storm was above-river.

Besides, she'd need her boot.

Jax tucked the pink plastic into the cross straps of his back-pack. He took out his expandable cane (which he hated) from a side pocket in his pack, and used it to stabilize himself as he hiked back uphill.

Progress was hard-won. His knee felt as if it was on fire. The blood stain on his pants leg had expanded, and Jax was beginning to feel light-headed. When had he eaten last? He couldn't remember. That couldn't be good.

The slope seemed to go on forever.

He couldn't stop. If he did, he might not have the energy to push on.

He was calf-deep in water when he saw the bridge. The raging torrent slammed against the bottom of the support girders. And the boards he'd stepped on to cross earlier? They bobbed in the current.

This was a bad idea.

And Jax didn't mean trying to cross the bridge. He meant his reason for being in Ecuador in the first place.

But what was he going to do? Return home and tell all the naysayers they were right? Turn his back on Owen and his dream?

Not a chance.

He'd take the bridge.

CHAPTER 3

TIFF and the nuns had just sat down to dinner and said grace when thunder rolled and someone knocked on the convent door.

The nuns all looked at Tiff, who shrugged and said, "It's not for me."

"*Gun,*" Sister Mary Rosa said in Spanish. There were no weapons in the convent. The nun had a nose like a bird dog. If she said gun...

A bolt of fear shot through Tiff. She'd heard about guerillas, mostly from her concerned friends in the states when she'd told them she was going to Ecuador. But she hadn't seen or heard anything about them since arriving.

"*What do we do?*" Tiff whispered. Hiding seemed a good option.

"*Answer the summons.*" Sister Mary Ofelia stood, and marched to the door to do just that.

Tiff held her breath as the nun opened the door. It tilted precariously, as if edging away from their visitor.

"*Hola.*" It was the wounded warrior—pale, drenched, and muddy, even the inside of his poncho. He clutched Tiff's boot in one hand and a cane in the other. Neither stopped him from doing a face-plant at Sister Mary Ofelia's feet.

"*It's for you.*" Sister Mary Ofelia pointed at the pink boot. "*Thank Saint Anthony.*"

Sister Mary Rosa pointed at the fallen soldier. "*Gun.*"

Tiff quickly moved to the man's side. Rain bounced off the second story wood deck, showering Tiff. "*He's still bleeding.*"

Sister Mary Lucia stood and pointed toward the supply closet down the hall. "*I'll get the med kit.*" Hunched over her cane, she looked like a black snail and moved at a snail's pace.

There was more blood on the man's pant leg than before. Tiff struggled to remove his backpack beneath his rain slicker so she could turn him over. His backpack was heavy, the poncho an annoyance. And then she saw his gun holster. She froze. She had no experience with guns and didn't want to shoot anyone accidentally.

"*Take his gun, child, and put it in the rice jar, point down,*" Sister Mary Rosa instructed. "*Then remove his rain gear.*"

Reluctantly, Tiff freed the gun from its holster and carried it to the rice jar with two fingers. She returned to the prone stranger and worked his slicker over his head, then slid the pack straps from his shoulders.

Towering above Tiff with her tall, bony frame and black robes, all Sister Mary Ofelia needed to pass for the Grim Reaper was a sickle. "*If he lives, he can't stay here.*"

The rain intensified, pounding the deck so hard water showered past Tiff, into the foyer, and onto the fallen veteran.

"*Of course, he's going to live,*" Tiff said. He was breathing deeply, although he looked as pale as death. "*You can't kick him out.*" Tiff pushed the cock-eyed door shut.

Sister Mary Ofelia made a door-stopper with her foot. "*The door stays open. Men aren't allowed in the convent.*"

"*It's nearly Christmas.*" Trying to keep her tone reasonable, Tiff glanced at the cross on the wall next to the shelf that held a carved wooden nativity. The house may have once belonged to Tiff's family, but now that the nuns had possession Tiff had to abide by their rules. "*You'll turn an injured man away?*"

The nun didn't bend. "*No men.*"

"*Why not?*" Something wasn't adding up. "*Just last week, Julio delivered firewood, stacked it in the corner, and stayed for lunch.*"

"*Julio is married,*" Sister Mary Rosa said cheerfully.

Sister Mary Door-Jamb shushed her.

"*And Enrique?*" Tiff continued, refusing to be bamboozled. "*He fixed the broken generator and shared our dinner.*"

Sister Mary Ofelia sniffed. "*Enrique is unified.*"

Tiff wasn't familiar with the term and asked for an explanation.

It was Sister Mary Rosa who answered. "*It is a free union, without having to pay for the paperwork of a judge and a civil marriage fee. The people here are so poor that as long as they come before God, we recognize their commitment.*"

The slow, shuffling steps of a returning Sister Mary Lucia echoed in the hallway.

"*Do you know him?*" Sister Mary Ofelia demanded.

"*Barely.*"

"*That's a shame.*" Sister Mary Rosa flashed the gap in her front teeth, exposing a missing molar as well. "*He could stay if you and he were unido.*"

The first unsettling tremors of trouble had Tiff clenching the wet doorframe behind her. "No."

She wasn't marrying a stranger just to bring him in out of the rain. She believed in love and happily-ever-afters. She just hadn't found the right man to commit 'til-death-do-we-part. She had five broken engagement rings to prove she'd been seriously looking and come embarrassingly close. Asking her to take part in a local marital custom when she didn't even know the man's name was ludicrous.

And if the press back home got wind of it...

"No," Tiff said again, louder this time, willing her hands to stop shaking.

"*Don't hesitate, child,*" Sister Mary Rosa said. "*This is why you're here.*"

Tiff shook her head. She'd come because Bon-Bon's chocolate supply had been compromised. They didn't have the money to buy enough quality cocoa beans to meet demand. And demand was sure to fall if they continued to produce average chocolate. Tiff was convinced re-establishing the family's plantations was the key to the company's survival. Her father was equally convinced she was wasting her time.

"*I have prayed for you and your purpose, child,*" Sister Mary Rosa said quietly. "*It's him. He needs you.*"

The most any man had ever needed from Tiff was the connection to the Bonander family and the promise of her inheritance. But this man...He wasn't looking to add to his investment portfolio. He wasn't looking to network in her social circles. He wasn't in need of her country club membership.

The troublesome tremors spread, making more than her hands shake. What if what Sister Mary Rosa said was true?

Okay, now you're just drinking the local Kool-Aid.

Still, Tiff leaned over him, taking in the dark stubble, the small scar near his ear, the scraped, sculpted cheekbones and the red, rising bruise beneath his eye. She tugged off his Dodgers baseball cap, revealing short black hair. She felt no love-at-first-sight excitement. No tingle of awareness in her belly. No fire of desire in her veins. There was only the premonition of trouble. He was just an average, down-on-his-luck guy she'd met in the forest. He wasn't her Prince Charming. End of story.

"*I cannot kneel.*" Sister Mary Lucia stomped her cane near the man's shoulder. Her reddish-brown freckles formed a bridge over her pinched nose. "*You will have to administer first aid and then send him on his way.*"

"*I'm not trained...I can't...*" Tiff glanced at his face again. It was a dependable, trustworthy face. She couldn't turn away. He needed assistance. That's why he'd come back this way. If the nuns weren't going to help him, she had to. "*Okay.*" She took a deep breath, took the med kit, and took a clinical look at him this time.

Black eye forming where he'd face-planted. Minor scrapes on his hands. His leg, the one that seemed to be bleeding (the one with the prosthetic she'd stomped on), twisted awkwardly. She set the med kit aside and tried to straighten his leg. There was a soft pop, similar to the sound of a jar opening. His prosthetic foot and calf came away in her hands.

Tiff gasped, but didn't drop the piece. Instead, she pulled it gently out of his wet pants leg. The concave top was blood stained.

The nuns crossed themselves, softly reciting prayers.

Why would he push himself to such limits? And why did she have the strongest urge to explore the texture of his hair? *"He isn't the reason I'm here."*

"Then we must ask him to leave when he awakens." Sister Mary Ofelia laced her fingers over her waist.

She didn't have to look so happy.

He groaned, shifting restlessly.

Tiff's gaze sought the most compassionate of her hosts.

Sister Mary Rosa shook her head. *"The decision is yours, child. We cannot compromise our vows or the sanctity of our home."*

JAX WOKE up to a strange sight. A penguin and an angel.

The angel he'd met in the rainforest. She sat on her knees next to him. Her mahogany hair fell in silken waves over her shoulders. "Snake Bait." In the light, there was a familiar quality to her face, although he couldn't quite place her.

The tall penguin...

A nun swam into focus. She leaned forward on her walker and smiled, revealing crooked, gapped teeth.

"Last rites?" he croaked.

"Unido," the nun said with an efficient nod.

Although he had no clue what *unido* meant—hopefully *not* impending death—Jax nodded and took stock of the situation as he'd been trained to do. His cheekbone throbbed. The pain in his knee had subsided to a dull ache. His head felt fuzzy, as if he'd been drinking. One eye was swollen shut. His clothes were wet and mud-stained. He could bolt, if need be. Not that where he was seemed a threat.

He was in a small room. Red and green curtains hung instead of cupboard doors in the kitchen area. A row of boots stood ready to march next to the wall, including a pair of pink flowered ones with a familiar machete hanging above it. The listing door was open to the rain. And his prosthetic rested in the umbrella stand near his feet. There seemed no need to run. It was just another day in the Ecuadorian neighborhood.

Hi. Welcome to our home. Let me take your fake leg.

"Hello," the angel said with an awkward laugh. "What's your name, sailor?"

"Jackson Hardaway." His voice still had that near-death, frog-like quality. "Army."

"Tiffany Bonander. New York." She had the prettiest smile, wide and reassuring. If it wasn't for the wrinkle in her slender brows, he'd have had no worries. "Do you know where you are?"

The rain let up, then intensified again, taunting him.

"Ecuador?"

"Good. Very good." Tiffany nodded too many times, like a school teacher acknowledging a student who hadn't given a precise answer. "Don't get up just yet. You passed out. You're in a convent." The tempo of her words sped up, like the flow of the tumultuous river he'd crossed. "I put salve and a bandage on your leg. But the world around us is flooding away. And in order for you to stay inside and not be washed away? We need to let the nuns do a little blessing. Are you good with that?" The wrinkle in her brow deepened, almost as if she wanted him to refuse. "Because you developed sores on your leg and you don't want to be out in the flood risking infection. It's very important that you understand, because the *unido* is a serious thing." Her whiskey-colored gaze slid from him, landing on her clasped hands.

"The *unido* is a blessing?" He glanced at his rolled-up,

bloodied, camo pants leg, wondering how much it would hurt to vamoose if *unido* referred to this country's local voodoo.

"A blessing, of sorts," Tiffany allowed.

"Then go for it."

Tiffany smiled in that way that both reassured and didn't. She said something in Spanish that made the nun look relieved. Then she took both his hands in hers. They were small, calloused hands that made him feel at ease.

The nun spoke in Spanish, raising her voice to be heard over the splashing raindrops. His command of the language was limited. He couldn't follow a word.

Tiffany's grip on his hands tightened. Her smile faded. She swallowed, looking everywhere but at him.

Freaky. "I don't hold hands on the first date," he joked, tugging his hands.

She didn't release him. In fact, she shushed him in a way reminiscent of the snake's hiss.

The nun stopped speaking and looked down on him expectantly.

"Say yes," Snake Bait hissed.

"Yes," he grumped. "Now can I have my hands back? This is starting to feel like a séance."

"Be still," Snake Bait whispered. Her touch cooled and heated him at the same time. When the nun stopped speaking again and looked at Tiff, she said solemnly, "Yes."

The nun concluded her speech with a flourish, crossed herself, and then kissed the cross about her neck.

Tiffany kissed each of his hands under the watchful eyes of the nun, and then released him. She stood and closed the door, muting the rain.

There was something oddly wedding-like about the blessing, but they hadn't asked him to say, "*I do*," or to kiss the bride, so he brushed the thought aside.

The nun wheeled out of sight. Jackson considered getting up, but his body was aching and it felt good to be horizontal, even if it was a hard, wooden floor.

"Welcome to the convent." Tiffany blew out a ragged breath as if she'd just survived a harrowing ordeal. "You've been invited to dinner, but you might want to clean up first. Do you need–"

"I'm not helpless." Anger jolted him to a sitting position. His head spun.

"I'm sorry. How should I say this?" Tiffany grimaced, then babbled in that non-stop way of hers. "Your clothes are wet and muddy. We have a bathroom down the hall where you can wash up and change. You can rinse out your clothes, but they may take a day or two to dry in this weather." She drew a quick breath, avoiding meeting his gaze. "What I was trying to say before was *do you need* to borrow some clothes?"

The anger drained out of him, replaced by humility. "It's my turn to apologize. People tend to treat me like I'm an invalid."

"Really." Tiffany stood. She'd changed into black yoga pants and a baby blue button-down. "No one who knows you would do that."

"That's what you think," Jax muttered.

She waved aside his sentiment. "You underestimate yourself, Tree-Hugger. We'll wait to eat until you're clean. It's safer for your feet if you keep a pair of shoes on while you're inside. I don't suppose you have a pair of flip-flops or slippers in your pack."

"No house shoes. I'll wear my boot." Using his arms for leverage, he got his real foot beneath him and stood. Tiffany handed him his cane. She still wasn't looking at him. *Why not?* "Just out of curiosity..." He waited until Tiffany met his gaze, and then gave her a mischievous smile. "What clothes would you have loaned me?"

Snake Bait didn't disappoint. One corner of her mouth turned up. "A nun's habit, of course."

CHAPTER 4

JACKSON HAD BEEN HERE LESS than two hours, and was already winning over the nuns. He'd changed into basketball shorts and a T-shirt. The nuns had helped him hang up his rinsed clothes, including several thin sleeves he put over his amputated limb.

Sister Mary Rosa patted his hand when he passed her the salt. Sister Mary Lucia kissed his cheek after he carried his dinner plate to the sink. And Sister Mary Ofelia? She smiled at the man as if she was sixteen, not sixty. All because he'd produced a small bottle of wine from his backpack.

Tiff should have gotten the nuns tipsy weeks ago.

"It's not a competition," Jackson whispered in Tiff's ear as they sat next to each other on a bench at the dinner table.

How did he know what I was thinking?

Tiff sniffed, ignoring the wisp of man-to-woman awareness that encouraged her to lean closer, to smile and let him know through the tilt of her chin and the batting of her eyelashes that she was interested. Because she wasn't. Despite the fact that they were in a poor-man's marriage. "I don't know what you're talking about."

"They're only pretending to like me best to make me feel welcome." One blue eye twinkled (the other being swollen shut).

He stretched out his arms and yawned. "Must be the *unido* blessing."

"Must be," Tiff muttered.

"And now, you will take him to bed," Sister Mary Ofelia announced, rising.

Tiff nearly fell backward off the bench. *"But—"*

The old woman tsked. *"He cannot sleep here alone."* She gestured for the other nuns to follow her down the hall. *"We go to pray."*

"You are unido now." Sister Mary Lucia pressed her freckled cheek briefly against Jackson's. *"It is a good thing."*

"I was right. He is your destiny." Sister Mary Rosa blew them a kiss as she wheeled her walker away. *"He is also your responsibility now, as you are his."*

Tiff swept a stray crumb from the table to the floor. Her body felt heavy and cumbersome. She turned to Jackson. She'd bound herself to this man—this stranger—out of kindness. Granted, it was in a ceremony unrecognized in her culture. But in the eyes of three holy women, they were married.

This is my wedding night.

She gazed down at her wedding trousseau. Flip-flops, yoga pants, and a wrinkled button-down. She finger-combed her hair, encountering tangles. According to the society pages, the Bon-Bon Heiress was quite a catch—a fashion icon, millions in her trust fund, and a lifetime supply of luxurious chocolate.

Those were the days.

Jackson stared at her with that half smile. "What's up?"

"It's time for lights out."

"Sure. Yeah." His smile faded. He must have picked up on her nervousness. How could he not? She was a wreck. "Just show me where I can bunk down. The floor out here works for me."

"No!" *Tone it down a notch.* "You need to come with me." Tiff handed him his cane, picked up his prosthetic, and then shouldered his backpack. She led him down the short hallway, and into her room. It was the same room she'd stayed in as a child.

"This is it." She put his stuff in the corner next to her cot with her pink sheet on it. All the luxurious trappings her grandparents had imported to Ecuador had been sold off long ago. "It's not exactly Trump Towers. It's not even the bed and breakfast my aunt runs in Cedar City, Utah."

Stop babbling.

"Is this your room? Am I putting you out?" Jackson leaned against the doorframe.

Across the hall, Sister Mary Rosa peeked at them, flashing her gap-toothed smile before closing her door.

"We need to talk." Tiff should have explained the situation when he'd first come to. She indicated he sit on a small folding camp stool in the corner. She closed the door and flipped the privacy latch. "*Unido* means we're...*friends.*" She was such a chicken. "We have to share a room."

Jackson pushed to standing. "Hey, no disrespect, but I'll sleep in the common room."

"You can't." She kept her back against the door.

He quirked a dark eyebrow over his good eye. "This is starting to get weird."

"I know, right? First the storm, then the snake, and now...*marriage.*" She tried not to cringe when she said it.

He didn't move, but his entire body tensed, like a boxer posing for a picture who was suddenly confronted with a real threat.

Tiff rushed to clarify, ending with, "So, if you can't share a room with me, you're out."

"I'm out." He moved with a hitching gait to collect his possessions.

Thunder boomed across the valley.

He sagged against the wall, his one good eye hooded. "On second thought, maybe I'll wait until they've gone to sleep, then sneak out to the common room."

"They'll hear you." She lowered her voice. "They're like ninjas. Silent feet. Ears like supersonic spy satellites. And don't get me started on their sense of smell. You can't get anything past them. Trust me, I've tried."

A few weeks back, one of the local farmers had offered to give Tiff a ride to the market in Guayaquil early one morning. Not wanting to wake the sisters, Tiff had gotten ready quietly. Sister Mary Ofelia had stopped her at the front door, asked her where she was going (and, more importantly, with whom), and saved her from all kinds of unpleasantness from the local pervert. She'd learned more than a few things about the nuns and the local farmers that day.

The thunder continued to roll.

Jax cleared his throat. "I'm trained in stealth tactics. I think I can get past three old women." He pinched the bridge of his nose, lost his balance, and fell against the wall.

Tiff helped him up. "Look, I'm not going to jump your bones, and I'm willing to take you at your word that you won't jump mine. I need the nuns, because I need to be here." She had nowhere else safe to stay. "*Please.*" She patted the folding stool. "Sit down, Jackson."

He sat, closed his eyes, and propped himself in the corner. "I prefer Jax."

"And I prefer Tiff." Before she realized what she was doing, she'd reached out and smoothed the furrow on his brow with her thumb. "We're going to go lights out, Otherwise the bugs, who have superpowers, will work their way through the screen or cracks in the wood. But first, I need to know a few things about you."

He cracked one eye open, a mere slit of Caribbean ocean blue. "Such as..."

"I'm not asking for your name, rank, and serial number." Or your cell number and social media addresses. "If I'm going to get any sleep tonight, I need to know something about *you*. Something...personal. It's not like we've just boarded a flight and I've strapped myself in for a little snooze while flight attendants watch over me. I'm going to sleep on the cot and you're going to sleep on the floor next to me."

"You want to put the stranger-danger issue to rest?" At her nod, Jax sat up straighter. "I reserve the right to refuse to answer."

"Fine." She perched on the edge of her cot and used her chirpy-cheerful voice, the one that said she had little in the brain department and was no threat to big, strong he-men. "What brings you to Ecuador?"

"I have a list of things I want to accomplish. Item one is a trek along the Andes."

He had a list of life goals. She had a daily to-do list. And most days she didn't even finish that. "You're hiking alone?"

"Obviously." His sarcasm was almost palpable.

Chirpy and cheerful morphed into serious and solemn. "How long have you been down here?"

"A week."

"And where do you call home?"

"Phoenix."

This was starting to feel like a police interrogation with a savvy, career criminal. She might have gotten more information if the storm hadn't moved on, because thunder clearly had an effect on him. "Any family?" *Wife? Kids?* Why hadn't she thought about that before railroading him into marriage?

"Just my parents and my kid sister." His eyes had a faraway look as he added solemnly, "My parents are disappointed in me."

"I find that hard to believe."

His gaze time traveled back to the present, pinning her. "Explain."

"I know what kind of *cajones* it takes to come to Ecuador. And I've got two legs." It was the truth, and she wouldn't take it back, although his expression turned grim. "My dad nearly had a coronary when I announced where I was going." And the reason. "Why would your parents be disappointed that you've taken on this challenge?"

"My family thinks I should be in a program for...a condition most vets are diagnosed with nowadays. It comes with four initials—starting with a P—and a slew of prescription meds. I don't want any part of it." Jax fell silent. He looked like a football player putting on his game face before the Superbowl. Tiff had no doubt that whatever was on his list of goals, he'd accomplish them all. "My parents think I've come down here to disappear. Or kill myself."

She nearly fell off the cot. "They may be your parents, but they seem to have misjudged you."

"All due respect, ma'am. You don't know me at all." His suddenly rigid shoulders. His suddenly formal speech. They both said: *back off*. But there was a sadness in his one open eye that contradicted all those boundary markers.

"*Au contraire.*" Tiff waggled a finger at him, attempting humor. "I know you want to avoid killing." Even a grumpy, hungry snake. "I know you can conquer those initials you refuse to acknowledge." P.T.S.D. "And I know you have a high pain threshold."

"Maybe not so high." That lopsided grin re-appeared. "I passed out on your threshold."

Honest, brave, attractive. She's always wanted to marry a man like that.

Oops. I just did.

"Okay, let me try another one. I know you're a gentleman." They may have just met, but she trusted him.

Tiff retrieved a rolled, woven reed mat from beneath her cot, shook it out, and spread it on the ground. "Thank you for making me comfortable. Lights out." She pulled the chain on the overhead light bulb and lay down on her cot, feeling very much like half of a couple in a 1950s sitcom, the kind where husband and wife slept on separate single beds. "Good night, my friend."

"Good night...*wife.*"

· · ·

A CONVENT. Nuns. An angel.

If his knee hadn't been an achy mess, Jax would've thought he'd died and gone to heaven.

The more he thought about it, the less upset he was over the *unido* ceremony. He certainly wasn't as upset as Tiff. Local customs meant nothing other than a roof over his head. It wasn't as if they were legally married. These ties wouldn't be binding.

Jax lay on the reed mat. He'd been in bathrooms larger than Tiff's bedroom. The shutter on the window was open, but no breeze came through the screen. The sounds of a passing storm rumbled in the distance drawing every nerve in his body taut. Angelic Snake Bait shifted restlessly on her cot and sighed. He could swear he'd seen her somewhere before. Her sweet scent reached him. Calm, comforting, sleep-depriving.

He had the oddest image of Tiff in his arms, smiling and whispering confidences. He could almost feel her body's warmth and the gentle press of her soft lips on his.

A pipe dream. All that pink and her dainty dinner manners. What would a woman like her see in someone like him?

He hadn't dated since his injury. How could he? He hadn't felt like a whole man.

He'd been a rough-and-tumble kid. Hunting? He'd load the rifle and take aim. Four-wheeling? Point him in the direction of the steepest trail. Sports? He was a sacrifice-your-body type of guy. Stitches. Sprains. Broken bones. Those injuries had made him feel *more*–stronger, more balanced, more masculine. A partial loss of a limb shouldn't make him feel deficient. With his prosthetic and time, he could do anything. But he did feel lacking, despite the fact that the rest of him worked just fine. If he didn't count the thunder-induced flashbacks, his slower pace, and his own self-doubts.

Since returning stateside, he'd been through the military-required group therapy. He'd even gone to a few individual sessions with a shrink. And he'd spent sleepless nights searching the war-darkened corners of his soul for answers. He'd found none.

His mother still cried when she saw the delicate pink tissue beneath his knee. He hadn't heard his father laugh genuinely since he'd come home from the V.A. hospital. His parents had put away the pictures of his youth. Not the toothy school mug shots or the posed family pictures. But the action photos of him playing football and soccer were gone. Nail holes on the wall were the only evidence of where they'd hung. Trace evidence, like the hole in his chest when he thought of that last day in Afghanistan.

Snake Bait blew out another sigh. Her matter-of-fact acceptance of his missing limb soothed the restlessness that had driven him to Ecuador months earlier than his physical therapist recommended. For the first time since he'd arrived, he felt he'd made the right decision.

CHAPTER 5

JAX MUST HAVE DOZED, because he startled awake to a rocket-like explosion. Except, instead of blinding bursts of light from a battle, the world was dark and temporarily at peace.

During skirmishes, silence wasn't to be trusted. He sucked in a muggy lungful of air. A scream coiled in his throat, spiraling toward release.

"You're all right." A small hand rubbed his right thigh, just above his knee and amputation. The scent of wildflowers drifted into his lungs, dissipating the urge to panic.

But his throat felt raw, as if... "Did I scream?"

"No." There was an odd note in that one syllable that didn't ring true. It angered him.

Outside, a howler monkey echoed his sentiment.

"It's not good to start a relationship with a lie, Tiff."

"I...you...You thrashed when the storm came closer." Those flat notes. How he hated them.

The walls seemed to take a step inward. "Did I scream?" *Don't do this to yourself, man.*

"It's the middle of the night. Let it go." Her voice should have soothed him. The darkness and the quiet should have soothed him.

"It's a simple question, Snake Bait." His jaw clenched tighter than a dog's on a bone. "Did. I. Scream?"

"If you must know..." She removed her hand from his thigh. "It was more like a primal howl."

Jax bit his lip, vowing to stay awake until the storm passed.

Thunder boomed above in rapid succession.

His body stiffened and jerked as if he'd flat-lined and been shocked back to life.

Her hand returned to his thigh. "That was the noise you made."

Criminy. He hadn't realized he'd made a sound.

"It's the thunder, isn't it? Do you want to talk about it?"

"No." If he was going to get through this—the residual of war, his body image issues—he needed to do it alone. On his trek through the Andes. Or somewhere else if that didn't work. He'd walk around the world until he felt like a man again.

"Well, I want to talk." She patted his leg. "The...uh...There is a...uh...population of small, sometimes large, insects that dislike rain. They always seem to know that my room is warm and dry. And they always show up after midnight."

A week ago, he might have chalked up her phobia to weakness. He'd since seen the size of Ecuador's bugs.

The first smattering of rain landed on the tin roof.

"Just so you know," she continued. "Big vibrations and light, even from a cell phone, draws them in from the cracks. It's the reason for early lights out and why I won't turn on the light for you."

"I don't need a night light!"

Her hand withdrew from his leg.

Thunder raged.

He gritted his teeth, determined to make no noise, determined not to speak, determined not to beg for her calming touch.

Noise filled the room anyway.

She was humming. It took him a moment to identify the song: *a lullaby*.

The heat of anger rumbled through his veins. Panic attacks. Nightlights. Lullabies. She must think he lacked a Y chromosome.

Thunder boomed strong enough to shake the convent's foundation.

Her hand returned to his thigh.

"I didn't howl," he snapped.

"Listen, my tree-hugging friend. I'm a city girl. Down here, there are no street lights. There's no noise from civilization—not angry taxi cab drivers, not upset protestors, not even passionate couples fighting in the apartment next door." Her fingers gripped his quad as her words ran together, filling the room with the tenor of panic. "At any moment, the creepy-crawlies are going to start marching through the cracks. They'll make an assault on my hair, because they seem to like it. I'm warning you now. I'll scream. And then the next time it thunders your moan will sound like a...well, a bedroom noise, and both our sounds will bring Sister Mary Ofelia pounding on the door, demanding silence."

Thunder shook the building once more.

She drew a shaky breath. "So let me be a girl and hang onto the nearest guy, even if he's such a tree-hugger he won't shoot a snake."

The world slowed. Tiff wanted *him* to protect *her* from the night terrors?

The irony made him laugh.

IT WASN'T every day that a girl promised to spend the rest of her life with a man. The least he could do was *not* laugh at her fears.

She'd broken engagements with men for less heinous acts. Reginald's night breathing had grated on her nerves. Wendell's snobbery was too much to bear. Adam's shoe addiction, Malcom's love of the nightlife, Chad's designs on the family business. None of it was personal. But Jax's laughter hurt.

That didn't change the fact that the bugs would be here soon. Tiff rolled onto her back on the cot, fingers clutching the sheet. She began humming her favorite lullaby, the one she used to sing to her baby brother when he couldn't sleep.

In the weeks since she'd been here, only a few storms of this intensity had rolled through. And every time, the bugs came marching in.

Her ears strained to hear the soft scratch of delicately hinged legs on wood. Instead, she heard Jax's breathing—slow and steady. Until the shudder of thunder destroyed its even cadence.

"Why are you here?" he asked raggedly.

"Good question." If the cocoa beans didn't dry properly, if they didn't taste good, all her efforts would be for nothing.

"Are you thinking of becoming a nun?"

"Not hardly." Not when touching a man—*touching him*—made her pulse beat an alluring tango. That rhythm made her forget she couldn't afford any more rash decisions regarding men.

Thunder rumbled in the distance.

"I answered your questions," he prompted in a voice tinged with desperation.

He was desperate? Was that scratching noise a bug? Her fingers knotted in the cotton sheet.

She swallowed back her fears, the same as she'd been doing for weeks. "I came here because my family owns all the cocoa fields in the valley. The Nacional cocoa tree from the Arriba region produces some of the richest chocolate in the world. But the variety isn't robust. It's susceptible to disease and produces a limited crop." Was that his foot scraping over the reed mat?

"Was there an answer in there?"

"No."

"Then I don't get it. Why are you here?"

Maybe if she hadn't been scared. Maybe if he hadn't laughed at her. Maybe if she didn't seem to understand Jax. Maybe she would have kept her mouth shut. "My father thinks that because I'm a woman–" And couldn't seem to make a relationship with a man work. "–that I can't manage the family business. He's wrong. He's wrong in more ways than ignoring the fact that buying cheap cocoa beans for our premium product means inferior taste. He doesn't believe I listened when my grandfather spoke. He doesn't believe I learned how to graft cocoa beans from a master when I came here for ten summers. He doesn't believe me when I tell him I can graft a cocoa tree that produces high quality cocoa beans in higher quantities than our original orchard." Her words were loud enough to bounce off the ceiling and pelt her with inadequacy.

What if she was wrong?

"Your magic beans," he said softly.

"They're not magic, they could be game changing! And my father doesn't see it because I've made a mistake or two–" Or five. "–in my personal life." She let go of the sheet and pounded the cot rail with her fist. "I need those beans I was carrying to prove I'm right."

Something touched her scalp. A thin, little something. Followed by a buzz of wings near her ear. She screamed and rolled off her cot onto him.

He grunted. She gasped.

Jax smelled of the dank forest, the green of the river, and man. He shifted beneath her. His body was lean and muscular. His grip on her arms strong as he steadied her. She wanted to be held. By him. All night. He was that sturdy. That real. Unlike the metro-sexual men she'd been engaged to.

The wings buzzed by her again. She rolled to his side with a shriek. "Get it off! Get it off!"

Sister Mary Ofelia banged on the door, her voice booming louder than the distant thunder. *"Show some respect!"*

Tiff buried her face in the crook of Jax's neck. "Oh, no. She thinks we're..."

His laughter rumbled in his chest. It was a nice chest. He was a nice guy.

Don't.

And yet, a warm feeling filled her. It was like coming home from elementary school and discovering freshly baked cookies. It was that feeling that had led her to accept marriage proposals, recruit bridesmaids, and inspire wedding watches on shows like Entertainment Tonight.

Her father's voice: *Can't you just be friends with a man?*

The chocolate chip cookie feeling dissipated.

The bug and Sister Mary Ofelia were gone. Tiff returned to her cot. She was glad Jax couldn't see her face. It felt hot enough to dry his laundry. "I'm sorry. It's just that the bugs...and you laughed at me..."

There was another awkward silence.

And then Jax spoke. "I laughed at the idea that you wanted me to protect you during a thunderstorm. I'm not very steady when it comes to thunder...I get...disoriented."

"I noticed." Her response was as small as her dismay over her misreading him was large. She had to learn to trust again. Amazingly, this man felt trustworthy.

"I'm here because I served in Afghanistan with a guy named Owen. His grandfather was from Ecuador." His words sounded creaky, as if they'd squeezed through barbed wire and been cut. "We were out on patrol when the ambush came. The bad guys trapped our unit on a rooftop. The missiles came as darkness fell and...a lot of guys didn't make it."

Including, she'd bet, his friend, Owen.

Tiff wanted to touch Jax, to let him know that in the darkness he wasn't alone. But he was temptation, and she always seemed to twist friendship into love, and then realize when the glow of shopping and planning the wedding faded that she'd made a mistake. She clasped her hands together over her chest and lay on her cot like a corpse ready for her viewing.

"Owen always talked about trekking through Ecuador along the Andes mountains like his grandfather had done." His voice had dropped to a whisper, one coated with regret and fringed with shaky determination. She'd been wrong earlier. He wasn't just an average man. He was an honorable man.

The knuckles on her fingers unlocked. One-by-one as if sequenced, her fingers unfurled. She reached down to touch his muscled thigh.

She'd been ostracized for her choices in men. She'd been vilified in the press for her public break-ups. But she'd never felt as alone as Jax sounded. "You're doing this to honor him."

"Yes."

Thunder drifted away. The rain let up. They didn't move.

"You and Owen must have been good friends," Tiff said.

He'd thought she'd been asleep. The storm had quieted long ago. Her hand still rested on his thigh. He wasn't sure anymore who comforted who.

"No." He might just as well admit it. "Owen was a rowdy, annoying idiot. He took too many risks until..." The end.

Sleeping in barracks, army tents, and hospitals, Jax had learned to gauge a man's mood by their breathing. Quiet meant relaxed. Uneven meant upset or hurting. Hyperventilating often meant go-for-your-throat rage.

Tiff barely breathed, barely moved, and concealed her mood as completely as the flood of water cascading down the narrow road outside. "Then why are you here?"

"Hokey as it sounds, we were a band of brothers." The temptation to cover her hand with his was strong. Stupid, but strong. They were strangers. It made no sense that he wanted to hold her and learn the texture of her hair and the taste of her lips.

If this was what one week in the jungle did to him...

Jax cleared his throat, and picked up his story, determined not to let his mind dwell on his hostess. "I didn't think much about Owen being an only child when we were deployed. But back in the world, in the hospital, I wondered who would trek for him."

The rain had stopped. The steady drip-drip as it came off the roof's edge made him tense. Or it could have been the fact that he wasn't telling the entire truth. Or maybe it was the dead bug in his hand. Its matchstick legs poked at his palm.

"It's an honorable thing." The soft, gentle cadence of her voice. She should have been a nurse. Her touch, her tone, her tolerance. They settled the restlessness within him.

"It would be honorable." He forced out the words. "If that was the only reason I was doing this."

"Don't tell me you need to prove you're a man?" Whatever compassion had been in her voice was replaced by humor. "I didn't think you were that insecure."

When he didn't say anything, she sat up. "You are." Her cot creaked. "This is interesting."

Jax gritted his teeth and tossed the bug beneath her cot.

"Why do men always need to prove themselves to the world?"

"Don't cast stones." A heavy one sat on his chest. "A few minutes ago you were going on about proving yourself to your father."

"To my father." And then she added in a less brazen, unconvincing voice, "Not to the world."

She was lying to herself and she knew it.

"If I had two legs, I wouldn't be doing this. I wouldn't have a list of things I need to...to...do." He'd be in Phoenix, sitting in an air conditioned, bug-free, snake-free living room, happy that he'd made it home in one piece. "I'm doing this to prove something to *me*. No one and nothing can keep me down, certainly not because I'm missing eighteen inches of bone. Who cares what my parents or the world think of me?" *Now who was lying?*

The Ecuadorian equivalent of crickets began chirping outside.

It was a fitting end to their ruse of a poor man's wedding night.

CHAPTER 6

"Merry Christmas. There's no running water." Tiff huffed back into her room the next morning, feeling every inch the put-out Bon-Bon Heiress. She and Jax hadn't talked since discussing their need to prove themselves.

She'd been telling herself for weeks she was down here to save the company and prove Daddy wrong. She'd conveniently refused to acknowledge that it would help her love-tarnished image if she succeeded in a legitimate endeavor. She was shallow. She wanted people, especially her father, to think highly of her. She wanted Jax to think highly of her. Was that such a bad thing?

Tiff stuffed her dirty clothes in her laundry bag. "Darn water pump is as temperamental as Sister Mary Ofelia."

Jax sat on her cot, changing the bandage on his knee. Nothing about him was posturing or self-conscious. The skin around his eye was black, but the swelling had reduced considerably. She could see two blue eyes, eyes that regarded her levelly. "Do you want me to have a look?"

The morning was bright and sunny, promising to be hot and muggy later on. Her morning shower was her one luxury, the one time of the day she wasn't hot and sweaty. If she lost that...She swallowed her pride. "Could you fix it?"

THE WEDDING PROMISE   43

He put on his boot. "I'll look after I get my bionic leg on." He could joke about his setback. Why couldn't she?

"Let's eat first." She led him to the common room.

In the kitchen, Jax fingered the wet material hanging over the hot plate. "My socks are still wet."

"It takes two days for clothes to dry in here. Three in my room." She was lucky her bras hadn't been drying in her room last night. How embarrassing would that have been?

"I wanted to leave today, but without dry liners..." Jax frowned, fingering a pocket of his cargo pants above his missing appendage.

She wanted to kiss his cheek and tell him not to worry. Okay, on a morning of self-examination, that wasn't quite right. Tiff wanted to kiss his worries away...on the lips. What was happening to her? "I'm sure the sisters would be happy to host you for the Christmas holiday." Once more, she swallowed her pride and decided to be honest. "I'd be happy if you'd stay."

Was she nuts? It was starting again. The attraction. The appeal of being part of a couple. The feeling that he was *The One*.

And yet, she babbled on like the flooded river. "Besides, you said the river crested over the bridge. Unless you try your hand at swinging on vines, you're not crossing today." Maybe not even until the day after tomorrow. Tiff hoped he'd stay until his knee healed. She kind of hoped he'd change his mind altogether and return home. Ecuador had daily rain showers. How did Jax expect to make it through a thunderstorm every day without freaking out? "It seems odd that you'd come out here at Christmas."

"I couldn't take it at home anymore. It'll make things easier for my parents, trust me." He sniffed the oatmeal Sister Mary Rosa had left on the hot plate. "Why aren't you home for the holidays?"

"I was supposed to spend Christmas with someone, but it fell through." She couldn't bring herself to tell him the whole truth. She was supposed to have married Chad on Christmas Day.

Lying, manipulating Chad, who was Greek god beautiful and Greek god vindictive. She dished Jax a bowl of oatmeal with a forceful flick of the spoon. "Why don't you sit at the table? I'll bring your food."

"Where are the nuns?" He limped toward the table, leaning heavily on his cane.

"Sit on the bench we sat on last night, not–"

Jax yelped and clutched at the table, having sat on the bench she was in the process of warning him away from.

"Are you okay? I should have spoken up sooner." She gave him a once-over. All his muscles seemed to be in their proper place. "One of the bench legs rotted and is crumbling. It's more like a rocking chair now."

He leaned over for a closer look. "You let the nuns sit here?"

"They insist." The elderly trio was a stubborn, independent lot. "And they insist on waiting for someone named Elvis to fix it."

"You're right. It's not exactly Trump Towers. Or your aunt's B&B. Where did you say that was?"

"Cedar City, Utah. The Iron Gate Inn. They get a lot of trade from the local Shakespeare Festival, plus their fair share of weddings. It's a beautiful place, right out of a history book." She put the brakes on her babble-mouth.

"You're cute when you gush."

Cute? She drew the compliment close, while simultaneously reminding herself not to get carried away.

Jax propped the bench upright against the wall and took a seat on the one they'd shared last night. "If you have some basic tools, I can fix that."

He'd need planked wood, something rare in these parts. She wouldn't burst his bubble just yet, not when she was hopeful for a water pump fix. "A plumber and a carpenter? It really is Christmas." He was too good to have been found wandering in the rainforest. "Might I point you in the direction of the front door? If you open it too quickly, the bottom will swing out on you."

She served up a bowl of oatmeal for herself, and carried both bowls to the table.

"Breakfast with a beautiful woman and a honey-do list. How quickly the honeymoon ends." He winked with his good eye. "Where are my hosts, wife?"

"Please, don't call me that." She sat on the bench next to him, careful to keep a respectable distance between them. She should tell him about the five rings in her jewelry box. But not only would that stop the wife-calling, it would erase any respect he had for her. "The nuns left early to go into the nearest village to give blessings and lead an early afternoon Christmas service."

Jax dropped his spoon in his bowl. "They all went? Even Sister Mary Rosa and her walker? On foot?"

"You're making me feel like I should be stopping them." No one stopped them. "Those women cling to their independence like a barnacle to a coastal rock. Besides, the bus service knows when they need a pick up. I heard it come by earlier. And it'll bring them home in time for Christmas dinner." It was practically door-to-door service.

"The bus?" His raised brows were lopsided due to his black eye. "But the roads must be impassable."

"They're more gravelly and quick-draining above the river." She stirred her oatmeal as if stirring it might reveal the answers to her questions. Or erase her need for acceptance. "What I said last night? About proving yourself as a man? I stepped over a line. You made me realize how important approval is to me, when it should be the least important thing."

It was his turn to stir his oatmeal. "We all tell ourselves little white lies to get through the day." He angled his head to look at her with his good eye, drawing her in with that intense gaze. "The thing that bothers me is that most people judge me based on my appearance."

"You mean your gorgeous, model-like features?" She scoffed. "You shouldn't be offended by the association. Models aren't all empty headed."

He flashed that lopsided grin.

"Seriously." She cleared her throat. "You don't need anyone who judges you by the number of toes you have."

"And you shouldn't care what the world thinks of you, either. You'll develop that super-strain of cocoa bean tree. But you should do it because it makes you happy, not because you're looking for something to make your dad proud."

"What a pair we make." She tried to make light of her insecurities. She was afraid she'd failed.

Jax placed his hand over hers on the table. "Who you are today matters. Not your past or your past mistakes."

If only that was true. She turned her hand to clasp his. Best to keep things light. "I got lucky when I married you, sailor."

Sailor. It was the nickname her grandmother had used for every boy with spunk. Jax had plenty of spunk.

"It's Army." He drew his hand away. "About that. Before I leave, I'd like the nuns to undo our *unido.*"

She nodded stiffly. Her first marriage and her first divorce. All in one week. Practically in one day.

Merry Christmas.

THERE WAS nothing like taking away a man's limb to make him feel inadequate. Add having to hop down stairs on one leg because his prosthetic socks were still wet, and Jax had to bite back his need to voice his frustration.

He may have talked a good game about not caring for anyone else's opinion, but he'd lied. He was bunny-hopping down the stairs followed by a beautiful woman. One he was married to. He might just as well belch and fart to complete the illusion that he was one heck-of-a-catch.

The moment he told Tiff he wanted out of their *unido,* he knew it was the wrong thing to say. Her smile had shattered and fallen to the floor. The more he got to know Tiff, the more it seemed wrong to stay in a relationship without love. And yet, it

felt wrong to sever their tenuous connection, because...because...
There was something about Tiff, something he was drawn to.

By the time he reached the bottom of the stairs, Jax was
sweating in his cargo pants and T-shirt. He used his cane like a
crutch to traverse the path to the rear of the convent where the
water pump and rainwater harvesting system were located.

Tiff trailed behind him, carrying a small toolbox. She'd
donned her pink boots, skinny jeans, a lime green button-down,
and a red bandana around her neck. She'd braided her hair.
When she'd been in the kitchen, the tail of her braid swung
across her shoulders when she walked, daring him to catch it and
draw her close, kissably close.

The heat's getting to me. "I haven't taken the place of anyone
special in your life, have I?"

Her laughter was short and hollow. "I'm on a sabbatical from
men."

"Been burned, have you?" Who would let her go? Only a
fool...like him.

"Something like that."

The sun was already baking. Around the clearing surrounding
the convent, the forest dripped and splatted as water made its
way down to the ground. The air had a green, fresh quality over-
laying the usual mugginess. They walked beneath the stilted
building where it was cooler, but it smelled moist and dank.

Jax tapped the gauge on the water pump. It read zero pressure. Not a good sign. Neither was the amount of rust around
the system.

Tiff had paused by a wood and wire rack. She inspected her
cocoa beans. "Too soon to tell if they're ruined." She joined him,
gesturing toward the pump. "Rust and mold. Welcome to life in
Ecuador."

"Could have been worse," he said.

"How so?"

"Owen could have wanted to trek the North Pole." He loosened the wing nuts on the pump cap so he could check the

connections. "I'd be freezing my remaining toes off." In which case, he never would have met her. Could he get away with taking his divorce request back? He could apologize. "About *unido—*"

The pump system began to buzz.

"What's that noise?" Tiff backed up a couple of steps.

"I don't know. It doesn't sound mechanical." He loosened the last wing nut and lifted the cap.

A bee flew at him, dive bombing and circling.

Tiff waved her arms, presumably trying to scare the bee away. "You made him angry."

"Bees are always angry." He tried to swat it.

It flew past his ear. And then there was silence.

"Ow!" Jax slapped the back of his arm, feeling a small body squish beneath his palm. "He stung me."

"Let me see." Tiff came around behind him. The top of her head barely reached his shoulder. "I want to make sure it wasn't a scorpion."

Jax went very still. "They have those here?"

"They have everything here." She gently pinched the skin of his bicep. "Got the stinger. You aren't allergic to bees, are you?"

"Never have been before. And I seem to be breathing okay. Although it stings."

Something soft and wet pressed against the sting. Immediately, he felt better. "What was that?"

"My grandmother's feel-better remedy." She moved beside him, brushing a lock of sweat-dampened hair from his forehead. "A kiss to the finger pressed to your boo-boo."

Boo-boo. Heat flash-fired unexpectedly through his veins. The term shouldn't have been a turn-on.

And suddenly, he got it. His attraction to her. Boo-boo or not, Tiff treated him like a man. Like a man she was comfortable with and respected. She didn't shudder at the sight of his stump or rush to open the door for him. He didn't need to walk the

Andes to prove anything to her. Tiff cared for him without him having ten toes.

She cared for him, didn't she? He couldn't be reading that wrong. She'd spent a long time last night with her hand on his leg. And they'd shared their secrets.

Tiff licked her lips, those plump, kissable lips. "Is something wrong?"

Everything was wrong. He'd met her less than twenty-four hours ago. If he kissed her, she'd think he was a one-night stand type of guy, especially since he'd essentially just asked her for a divorce.

He dragged his gaze away from her and peered into the pump. "There's a nest in here." He cleaned it out. Almost immediately, the gauge went from zero to thirty-two pounds of pressure. The pump was equalized, but his heart was chugging in the red zone. "You should have water pressure now."

"Impressive." She grinned, not helping slow his heart rate.

He tried not to grin back like a lovestruck idiot. "Hey, I took one for the team. You should be impressed." He replaced the lid.

"It was a bee sting, not a scorpion strike. Let's check out the bus stop." She lifted the tool box and led the way this time, walking at a good clip instead of at a slower, handicapped aide's pace.

You'd only resent her if she did.

Jax smiled and hustled after her. It was a fairly clear path. The undergrowth had been trimmed raggedly on either side. "Who cuts back the jungle? Not Sister Mary Ofelia."

"Usually one of the men from the village. I've been doing it since I arrived." She patted the machete hanging from her belt. Tiff was an appealing contradiction of New York polish and gutsy frontier woman. She stepped out onto the road and into the full sunlight. It danced off her brown hair. She shaded her eyes, glancing up and down the road. "I'll never get used to how fast the rain dries up around here. Across the river it'll be muddy for another day or so."

Jax moved beside her. The road was muddy, no longer a shallow stream. He glanced at a tilted mess of wood planks and tin. "I take it they don't set posts in concrete for stability."

"Nope."

"If we had some bamboo to sink as posts, this thing wouldn't collapse." All those DIY projects he'd done with his dad were coming in handy today.

"I can cut some bamboo." Tiff gestured to a bamboo cluster across the road, and withdrew her machete.

Standing in that shaft of sunlight, holding a weapon, she was beautiful. She was also intelligent, compassionate, and independent. His heart was in big trouble here.

She raised a dark, slender brow. "Are you feeling okay? That's the second time this morning you've gotten a funny expression on your face."

He'd seen his comrades look goofy when they fell for a woman. Only made sense that he'd look the same. Not that he could tell her he was falling for her. He scrambled for an acceptable response. "I was just trying to calculate the length of bamboo we'll need." *Good save.* "I'm thinking about eight feet. While you're doing that, I'll see about salvaging what I can from this mess." *And think of a way to tell you how I feel.*

Was he nuts? He hadn't even kissed her.

She turned, surveying the trees.

A clump of greenery caught his eye in the tree above them as she stepped away. "Wait."

Her shoulders tensed. "What is it? A snake? A spider? Is it on me?"

"It's mistletoe." He pointed above them. "You know what that means."

She glanced up, her cheeks blooming as softly as that wild-flower scent she wore. "That's not mistletoe."

"Come here, wife." He held out his hand. "You can't be *unido* without a kiss."

She swallowed. Her cheek color deepened to a dusky rose. "You wanted an annulment."

"I haven't had my coffee today. I was out of my mind." He would be if she didn't kiss him. "Forgive me."

"Jax, I – "

"We've survived a snake stalking, a flood, and a thunderstorm. Kiss me, Tiff. Kiss me like the vows we agreed to yesterday mean something." He limped toward her, not caring that his movements weren't smooth. This was Tiff. She wouldn't care. "All these signs mean we're meant to be together."

She didn't move. Not to encourage him. Not to ward him off.

That was a good thing, wasn't it? "Do I have to do everything myself?" he whispered. "You won't meet me halfway?"

She swallowed again, her gaze on his lips. She wanted that kiss. She wanted *his* kiss.

He closed the distance between them with another suave hop-step.

His hand to her cheek. "So soft." His thumb to her lips. "So warm." His nose met hers. "So sweet."

"Jax, I...*Jax?*"

He'd drawn away. "That was an Eskimo kiss. *Unido* sealed." He began to turn away.

"That was no kiss." Ah, the fire in her tone.

He worked his jaw to prevent himself from smiling. "It was."

"No. This is a kiss." She grabbed his T-shirt and tugged him close. Her lips claimed his. Urgently. Possessively.

She was everything he'd expected – sweet, passionate, a spark that ignited his flame. He dropped his cane and slid his hands around her waist, negating the empty space between them, negating the emptiness inside of him.

He blazed a trail with his lips across her cheek and down the slender column of her delicate throat.

Her breath was as ragged as his, except she had enough oxygen to speak. "Oh, Jax." She sounded like an angel.

He nipped at the smooth skin at the base of her neck.

"Oh, Jax." She sounded like an angel about to fall completely and utterly in love.

He worked his way back up to her ear.

"Oh, Jax." She stiffened and screamed. "There's something in my hair." She spun in his arms. "Get it out. Oh, get it out!"

Sure enough. It was a bug. A big purple dragon fly, legs tangled in her braid. He freed it. And when he did, Tiff hurried across the road and began hacking bamboo.

"Come back here, wife."

She didn't answer.

And she didn't look back.

CHAPTER 7

AN HOUR after cutting bamboo posts, building a new lean-to, and not talking about that electric kiss, they headed back to the convent. Tiff carried a leftover board Jax thought he could use to fix the dining room bench, and the shovel she'd used to dig post holes.

She shouldn't have kissed him. She fell in love with the speed most people decided to try the daily special. She couldn't put Jax through the microscope that was her life in the states. And she couldn't risk encouraging him only to hurt him later. She liked him. She liked him far too much. And his kiss...He had mad skills. But in this case, it wasn't him that was wrong for a relationship, it was her.

"I wish you would've let me dig the holes," Jax said for the umpteenth time. A complaint infinitely preferable to him asking what he'd done wrong when they'd kissed.

She didn't break stride ahead of him. "Don't tear up your man card just yet, Jax. I don't mind hard work." He started to say something else, but she cut him off. "And before you tell me it makes you look weak, may I remind you how hard it is to balance on one leg and a cane while wielding a hammer? You burned more calories than I did."

He sighed. It was an endearing sigh, one of capitulation. "I bet you don't let guys open doors for you, either."

"You'd be surprised what I let guys do when I'm wearing four-inch heels." She put the shovel back with the other tools beneath the convent, and propped the plank against a stilt. It was hot and she was a damp, sweaty mess. She untied her bandana, lifted the braid from her shoulder, and wiped the sweat from her neck and face.

Jax caught up with her. He walked slower without his pros-thetic, but he wasn't winded. "If wearing four-inch heels means you let a man kiss you, please tell me you have skyscraper heels upstairs."

Hair still held to her crown, she glanced over her shoulder at him. "No."

"Oh, my God." Jax grasped her arm and turned her around. "I just realized where I'd seen you before. You're the Fleeing Fiancée. The Bon-Bon Heiress. The Runaway Bride."

Her cheeks heated. "Don't forget the Bon-Voyage Bride, the Goodbye Bride, and the Fanciful Fiancée."

"A Bonander from Bon-Bon Chocolates. My mom used to buy me a Bon-Bon Bunny every Easter." He laughed. "I'm trip-ping. You're a celebrity. And you're here. In the wilds of Ecuador."

"Yep, I'm here," Tiff deadpanned, wishing a bug would fly in her hair again.

Jax was still in recognition mode, putting the pieces together. "I saw you in People when I was overseas. Someone had taken your picture as you fled down the church steps. Your hair was up, like you just had it. And wow." He wiped a hand behind his neck. "Isn't this awkward?"

"For me, yes." She maneuvered the plank between them.

"You must have been engaged to a lot of guys to earn all those nicknames." He spoke slowly, as if choosing his words carefully. He was probably regretting that kiss.

Smart man. "You must have seen me in more than one magazine to know so many of my monikers." She couldn't hide her bitterness. Each gossip magazine created their own nickname for her. Headline writers must be paid by the cheese factor.

He nodded. "I was in the hospital for quite awhile. I needed something light to read."

"Why didn't you read a sports magazine?" Why wasn't he running for the hills? Didn't he realize she was the ultimate relationship tsunami? She created chaos in the lives, and broke the hearts, of the men she'd loved.

"Are we arguing about gossip magazines?"

Tiff sealed her lips, refusing to feel embarrassed by her past. What was it he'd said earlier about the white lies people told themselves?

"We are." His voice was filled with wonder. His mouth curved in that familiar half-smile "This is our first fight."

"I believe we've been fighting for the past twelve hours about the need to prove ourselves to others." He'd wanted to annul the *unido*. Now he had a good reason to. She spun away, heading toward the stairs. "Go ahead. Say it."

"Say what?"

"That I led you on when I kissed you. That you can't trust me or my feelings given I've already broken so many engagements." She reached the bottom step.

Somehow, he'd kept up with her. He caught her arm. His grip was firm, but tender. Or maybe she was deluding herself again.

"Don't tell me men have said that to you before." A whirl of anger and frustration vibrated through his words like the buzz of that bee. "Or is this what you expect of men? Of me?"

"Isn't it obvious? My own father thinks I'm a flake. Why would any man I'm interested in think otherwise?" She tugged her arm free. "How can you be sure the feelings I think I have for you are real? How can you...when I...?"

"Can't even trust yourself?" He rested his palm over her cheek. "Haven't we been talking about believing in ourselves? Everyone has doubts, but it takes trust and faith to commit."

"Haven't you heard anything I've said? The stories about me are true. I fall in love and then I bail." It pained her to say it out loud.

He pressed a brief kiss to her lips. "Those men didn't know you. They knew Tiffany Bonander with her Fifth Avenue fashion and her four-inch heels. That's not the entirety of who you are."

"You don't get it." Tiff was tired. Tired of ending things. Tired of pretending she didn't hurt when she closed a relationship. Tired of this empty feeling that she was destined to be alone. "Don't, Jax. Trust me when I say that odds are I'll break your heart."

"Tiff, the only way that's possible is if you accept it first. Slow down. We've only just kissed."

She felt ill. Her hand drifted over her stomach. "We committed to something in there last night. I know it was without your consent. And everything would have been fine if you'd only kept it platonic. But now there's something more and I'm not the follow-through type of girl." She ran upstairs, unable to face him any longer.

She pushed the slightly ajar door all the way open, righting it before taking off her boots and putting on flip-flops. Time for a change of subject. "I bet this board is the perfect size for that bench," she said when he limped into the doorway. That was another problem. He shouldn't seem so strong and masculine walking around on a cane.

She sighed. It wouldn't matter what he looked like—handsome or homely, muscular or weak. He was Jax and she found every fiber of his being, every thread of his personality, appealing. She was so screwed.

"How many times have you been engaged, Tiff?"

"Do we have to do this?"

"Yes." He was persistent.

"Five."

"So this is the first time you've been married? That means something, don't you think?"

"It means I didn't want to turn you out into the rain." She held the board to the bench, but she didn't really see it. She was remembering Chad's face when she'd bolted out of their engagement party. He'd looked hurt, and then angry. So very angry. And the aftermath? He'd sold every private moment they'd shared to the highest bidder, complete with pictures. "My last fiancé claimed I was incapable of love."

"You can't believe that." His voice was a husky growl of disapproval. "You shouldn't believe that. I certainly don't." He took two steps into the room. "What happened Tiff? I'm not asking for a blow-by-blow. But you're down here in Ecuador with nothing but hard work to fill your days. That leaves a lot of time to think."

"I..." She shouldn't tell him. She wouldn't tell him. She blew out a breath and told him. "The falling in love part is easy. New York is a whirlwind of parties and nightlife. It isn't until the everyday happens that I'd realize we were wrong for each other."

"That sounds like a healthy perspective."

"Why couldn't I have that perspective in the first place?" Before the hoopla.

"It's called experiencing life and learning from your mistakes."

Tiff was silenced by the logic of his words. And yet, she couldn't truly believe them.

Jax took the board from her and sat on the table, lifting the broken bench from its resting place against the wall. "I think you're right. This will be a good fit. Hand me the hammer and some nails, would you?"

That was it? He wasn't going to try and convince her he was right? What was happening here?

She drifted to the hot plate on the counter and his clothes hanging above it. The sleeves that protected his knee were almost dry. She turned to tell him.

And that's when she saw the snake.

· · ·

Jax should have been used to Tiff screaming by now.

He wasn't.

She was backing up, shrieking and pointing at his feet. Her cry of terror morphed into a word. And the word sounded an awful lot like, "SNAKE!"

Jax leapt forward, landing on three limbs, before pivoting into a stand, using the wall for balance. The reptile in question was only a foot long, but it was red, black, and white. A coral snake.

With a visible shiver, Tiff backed up until she was close enough to grab his arm. "I put your gun in the rice jar on the shelf."

"I'm not killing that snake. It's just a baby." Deadly though it might be.

"I hate you, Tree-Hugger. We're getting a divorce." She shimmied around the way his kid sister used to do when she was waiting to get into a bathroom.

"Quit your potty dancing." The coral snake slithered under the table. "See? It's more scared of us than we are of it."

She muttered something about fools and their manhood, grabbed the bench, and used it as a broom to sweep the snake out the door and over the edge of the deck. "It'll be back." Tiff shuddered again. "They always come back. That darn broken door doesn't keep anything out."

"Can I save you every once in awhile?" Using his cane, he closed the distance between them and put his arms around her. She didn't hesitate. She melted into his embrace, smelling of wildflowers and sweetness. "Tiff, have you ever thought that you don't belong in Ecuador?"

She nodded, clutching him tighter.

"You should go home. It's Christmas Eve."

She shook her head.

"Why not?"

"The chocolate. My grandfather's legacy." She spoke into his chest. "And...I was supposed to get married tomorrow."

He felt the distinct urge to ring someone's throat. "Regrets?"

"No."

He shouldn't have been surprised at how relieved that made him feel. "Good."

"Good?" She lifted her head and met his gaze.

He couldn't help himself. He kissed her.

KISSING JAX and being in his arms felt right. The way a peanut butter and jelly sandwich felt right. The way a great pair of jeans felt right. The way no man had felt right before.

Tiff sighed and snuggled closer, letting Jax deepen the kiss.

The door tilted precariously once more. Sun slanted through the partially open shutters. A bird sang a lilting song. It was a regular day in Ecuador and she feared she was falling in love again.

Her father would have said it was because they'd survived two snake events together.

Her mother would have said it was because she was a sucker for a handsome face.

Her brother would have ruffled her hair and said she should move in with the guy before agreeing to marry him.

She'd disagree with all of them. But the fact remained—she'd made bad decisions in the past and five men had been hurt in the fallout.

Jax stroked her hair. His hand came to rest at the end of her braid. One tug. Two. He broke off the kiss. "You think too much."

She drew back to meet his intense blue gaze. "I'm thinking that starting anything with me is a bad decision on your part."

"Too late." He framed her face in his hands and claimed her lips again. No warning. No signals. No lack of skill.

His kiss. She sighed. Not too hot. Not too intense. Not out of control. Something inside Tiff eased, shifted, tilted toward

Jax–the man, his honorable heart. How she hoped she wouldn't hurt him.

All her tilting set them off balance. They caught each other. His cane fell to the ground.

His dark brows lowered, as if their pitching bruised his fragile male ego.

Tiff was quick to stop that nonsense. "That kiss knocked us both off our feet, sailor."

"I keep telling you. I'm Army." Humor did the trick. The impending storm was averted. His gaze softened and focused on her mouth. "I know you've kissed a lot of frogs, but maybe you can remember that."

She didn't think she'd ever forget. But jokes aside, she had to be honest. "Before this goes any farther, you have to remember that I'm the Bon-Voyage Bride, and the Fleeing Fiancée." And a long list of other titles.

His thumb stroked over her cheek. "You don't call yourself any of those names, do you?"

"No."

"Then I won't either."

She stepped free of his embrace. "Jax, I suck at relationships."

"Only if you can't learn from the past." He walked back to the table.

He was so hopeful. She was so very scared. "It always seems to start with a bang and then fizzles."

Jax pried the rotted wooden bench leg free. "Was there a bang when you saw me?"

"You shot your gun," she pointed out.

"There was screaming when you first saw me." His back was to her. She couldn't see his smile, but she felt it in his voice. "The bang came later."

He was right. At first glance, she'd thought he was a zombie. And then when he'd passed out in the foyer, she'd thought he was average.

"Remember how during *unido* I told you I don't hold hands on the first date?"

"Yes, but what does that have to do with my fickle heart?"

"It means we go slow. It means we talk through our feelings. It means we don't panic and bolt at the first obstacle." His voice was steady, no trace of recrimination or irritation. "Do you think you can do that, wife?"

She wanted to say yes. But fear clamped its hand over her mouth. Fear that she'd disappoint her family. Fear that she'd hurt Jax. Fear that she'd miss out on something that was real this time because she was too scared to commit.

CHAPTER 8

THE NUNS RETURNED in the late afternoon, full of holiday cheer, looking spent but happy. Their smiles broadened when they saw Tiff had prepared dinner and Jax had fixed the bench and door.

"They're gushing about the bus stop and water pump, too," Tiff translated. She met his gaze and then hers slid away, as if she was uncomfortable with him.

That had to change.

Jax and Tiff had spent a quiet afternoon puttering around the convent, never speaking more than was necessary to fix things that had been neglected.

Jax refused to classify kissing Tiff as a mistake. She may be afraid of what was blossoming between them, but he wasn't. Her lips fit perfectly on his. She knew exactly how to make him feel relevant. Back home, his parents barely let him get up to use the bathroom solo. Here, Tiff treated him like a capable man.

Since he'd suggested they go slow, Tiff had been standoffish. He'd be a fool to believe that anything lasting could exist between them. Forget her track record. They came from two different worlds. Her family was rich and famous. She'd been featured in gossip magazines. He tried to imagine her as the bridezilla the press made her out to be. He couldn't. Call him a fool. He thought they had a chance at something important.

Sister Mary Rosa had brought back a simple wreath made of thick green vines bound with strips of bamboo shoots. She wanted to hang it on the wall above a small shelf with a wood-carved nativity set. Jax obliged. The nun flashed her gap-toothed grin, and said something in Spanish to the other nuns that made them laugh, and Tiff blush.

"Want to translate that for me?" He cocked an eyebrow at Tiff, who was busy finishing dinner preparations.

"No."

He crossed the room, coming to lean on the counter. "Come on. Spill."

"They said..." Her pink cheeks turned a shade of red that made him want to kiss her again. "They said if you were this handy around the common areas, you should know what you're doing in the bedroom."

His head snapped around to regard the nuns. They sat at the table, tittering as they separated colorful embroidery thread. "That's not really what they said."

Tiff nodded. "I think they had wine after the service."

It was a different atmosphere than the night before, truly a jolly Christmas Eve. The sisters kept singing snatches of Christmas carols in Spanish. There was a serious note as they clasped hands at the dinner table and Sister Mary Ofelia led a prayer, but then it was back to smiles and a tumble of Spanish words.

After a dinner of rice, flat bread, and vegetables, Tiff fried plantains and topped them with sugar and cocoa powder. As Tiff was cleaning up the dessert dishes, Jax said, "I'd like to renew our *unido* vows."

She stiffened. "Why?"

"Because once upon a time you wanted a Christmas wedding and I'm leaving in the morning."

"All the more reason not to do this." There was suspicion in her voice, and maybe a hint of fear in her whiskey-colored eyes. "I don't want you to get hurt."

"I won't get hurt if we go slow." *Liar.* "More importantly, you won't get hurt if we go slow."

"Me?"

"Five broken engagements and not a word about your broken heart in the gossip magazines? You're not cold, Tiff. You didn't dump those guys and walk away unscathed. You believed you were making the right decision. I know you." He pushed a lock of hair from her face. "You're the woman who's brave enough to come to a foreign country alone and try to save her family's business. That's not the kind of woman who tosses a man's affections aside with a cold heart."

A tear slid down her cheek.

He brushed it away. "We'll take it slow."

"We won't see each other for months." Her gaze dropped to her feet and her cute toes. "Unless you stay."

"Stay?"

Her chin came up at the incredulity in his voice. "Your sores can't be fully healed. Don't ask me for time if you can't give it to yourself."

"I'll be fine." He rested his hand at the nape of her neck and rested his forehead on hers. "You'll get used to the idea of me—of us—while I'm gone. When I've finished this trek, you won't be scared of what's between us."

"Are you sure?" She glanced up at him tentatively.

"I have a feeling, deep down in my heart, that you're the only woman for me." He drew back. "So are you in for another round of *unido?*"

She hesitated.

"It would make the nuns happy." Not to mention Jax.

"The nuns are drunk. They've been sipping from a flask since they returned. If we renew our vows, they'll think we're..." She drew a breath. "They'll think we've taken a liking to each other."

"I've taken a liking to you." His gaze traveled her curves and came to rest on her lips.

"If your mother was here, she'd warn you away from me. She'd tell you that I make bad decisions regarding men." Her voice dropped below the hymn the nuns were singing until he had to strain to hear her. "She'd predict I'd break your heart."

"I know better."

Her face pinched up.

This just wouldn't do. "Sisters? Sisters?" He interrupted their hymn, pointing from Tiff to himself and back. "*Unido.*" He captured Tiff's hands with the hand that didn't hold his cane, and led her beneath the wreath. "Explain what I want—a gift for you at Christmas, a promise for the new year."

She sighed, but translated.

Sister Mary Ofelia's gaze softened. Sister Mary Lucia clapped her hands. And Sister Mary Rosa's gap-toothed smile spread from ear to ear.

"This feels too much like an altar." Tiff had taken her hair out of its braid sometime earlier. Her brown locks were thick and wavy, spreading over her shoulders like a rich curtain of chocolate.

"Consider it practice for the real thing," Jax whispered. "The things in life that are worth waiting for are worth working for. Like kisses and lasting relationships."

Her tentative smile made him forget he had physical challenges, that he'd be fighting labels the rest of his life, like handicapped and cripple. It made him forget her reputation and her prediction of failure. He was lost in the warmth of her hands, the growing solidity of her smile, and the soft acceptance in her eyes.

Sister Mary Rosa stood before them with her walker and spoke in lyrical notes Jax couldn't translate. Except he understood. She was asking if he'd love, honor, and cherish the woman next to him. He did all those things.

When the nun paused, looking at him expectantly, he said, "I do," instead of yes.

Tiff's hands convulsed on his. "What are you doing?"

"Practicing." His grin felt wider than the bridge downhill.

When it was Tiff's turn, she hesitated, turning questioning eyes to Jax.

"It's just me," Jax said, adjusting his balance on his cane. "It's just Christmas in a convent in the middle of nowhere. It's not legally binding." He didn't add it was emotionally binding. No matter what happened from this point on, he'd always feel bound to Tiff.

"I do," she whispered.

The nuns applauded and gestured at them to come together. To kiss.

They turned to face each other. He was smiling. She was not.

He kissed her anyway. A gentle kiss. A press of the lips so tender she'd know that he was willing to wait for her to gain her confidence in him. In them. But he couldn't resist pulling her closer, pivoting slightly on his good leg.

The nuns screamed.

Jax righted them. "I've never been to a country where people scream so much."

Tiff's eyes had widened. Her shoulders were hunched to her ears. "It's on my back."

"What?" He tried to lean forward to look as Sister Mary Ofelia handed him a water pitcher with a dish towel shoved in it.

"A spider. Sister Mary Rosa said it must have come from the wreath." Tiff did a mummy-turn, as if her feet were wrapped tightly together.

Jax gasped. Since starting his trek, he'd seen gargantuan snakes. He'd had bugs the size of tennis balls land on him. But this? It was a wolf spider – white and brown, hairy, and as big as his hand. It was perched halfway in Tiff's hair and halfway on her shoulder. "Poisonous, right?"

Tiff barely nodded. The nuns clutched one another and prayed with an intensity that made him nervous.

"I've got this." He forced confidence in his voice. What a mighty warrior he was. He'd been standing right there when that big, nasty spider had hopped down on his Christmas bride.

Sister Mary Lucia made a scooping motion, apparently indicating the spider would hop right in if encouraged by the pitcher. This was followed by a sweeping motion, possibly indicating that he should then cover the pitcher with the tea towel and hope it wouldn't get angry, be uncooperative, and sink those tarantula-like fangs into Tiff's flesh. Or hop out and onto him.

He'd rather it attack him than Tiff.

"Don't hesitate," Tiff whispered. The fear in her voice silenced the nuns.

Jax wished he had time to put on his prosthesis. Balance was called for. He set his cane on the table, fisted the tea towel in his left hand and gripped the pitcher handle with his right.

Scoop and cover. Scoop and cover.

"When I set this gentleman free outside, you're going to owe me a kiss," he said.

"I'll kiss you a second time if you kill it."

So tempting. "We'll see. Hold still." *And pray I don't fall over.*

The capture was anti-climactic. The spider didn't try to get out from underneath the tea towel. Sister Mary Ofelia took it outside.

Tiff collapsed into Jax's arms.

"One thing about Ecuador." Jax tightened his arms around her. "It's never dull."

MIDNIGHT. The revelry was over. The nuns shuffled to bed. There was nothing left to clean up.

It was Christmas Day. Come sunrise, Jax would leave.

Tiff's heart ached at the thought.

"Is the wildlife always so prevalent here?" Jax followed her down the hallway to her room. "Or is it because it's Christmas?"

"It's part of daily life. It still freaks me out, though." She closed the door behind him and spread the reed mat on the floor. "Thank you for a memorable holiday."

Jax sat on the mat by balancing on his cane. He patted a space next to him. "Come sit with me so we can talk without me getting a kink in my neck."

Tiff turned out the light and sat next to him. "It's not very comfortable." But the narrow cot wouldn't hold them both.

"It's better lying down." He stretched out, gently tugging her along with him.

How easy it was for Tiff to believe that this could last when his arms were around her. "This tops the Christmas when I got Barbie's Dreamhouse."

"Do you know what I like about you?" Jax pressed a kiss to her forehead.

"My ability to remain calm in a crisis?" Tiff let her hand roam over his chest.

"I like your ability to scream a warning in a crisis, sure." There was laughter in his voice. "But what I really like...*What I love*—"

She gasped and tried to sit up. "This is your idea of slow?"

He held her close. "Hey, I went through two *unido* ceremonies and captured a gargantuan spider for you. I'm allowed the use of the L-word as long as I don't use it in a short string of three words starting with I."

"Oh." She was let down. She shouldn't be.

"Don't change the subject." He stroked her hair. "I was talking about what I loved about you."

"If this is a top ten list, I'm not interested."

"I love—" he said louder. "—that you face your fears. Snakes and spiders and bees, oh my."

Jokes? That wasn't so bad. She snuggled closer, resting her hand over his heart. "You can go on."

"I know this thing between us scares you, but it can't kill you." His tone was resolute, like a politician giving his victory speech. "You've come a long way since your last break-up. You seem like you're in a good place."

"In a convent in Ecuador."

"I'm not kidding." He pressed another kiss to her forehead, making her sigh. "Can you see me in your future?"

She felt his question rumble through his chest. Her fingers over his heart seemed to absorb his vulnerability and his sincerity. She could see herself waking up to his lopsided grin. Hear him singing their babies to sleep. Feel the strength and confidence as he held her hand in good times and bad. "I can." There. She'd said it. "But what if you snore? What if we fight about where to live? What if—"

"Quit jumping ahead. It's like climbing a hill. You go one step at a time."

"Jumping ahead is what I do." It's why she was single.

"It's what makes you panic. Don't jump." He turned to whisper in her ear. "When you get scared, remember us like this. Remember that we're in this together. We'll move forward together."

"If that were true, you'd stay until your sores are fully healed and we've had more time to settle into this."

Now it was Jax who stiffened, Jax who sounded boxed in. "I have additional padding for my knee. I can make it to Quito. Don't ask me to stay because you doubt me."

"I'd never ask you to cancel your trip. I know how important it is to you." Her fingers had curled around the collar of his T-shirt. "And I'm not doubting you'll make it on pure will power. I'm asking you to wait until you're ready. Where will you stay every night? If you sleep in the open, the bugs will eat you alive." She forced herself to pry her fingers free, smoothing the soft cotton. "And the thunderstorms..."

"Owen's grandfather trekked from Guayaquil to Quinto. If he can do it, I can do it." So determined. So proud. "He walked because his love moved to Quinto and her father refused to let them marry. He figured if he walked the entire way that he'd earn the man's respect. And he did. You have to see why I have to do this."

"I do," she murmured, unable to quell the fear she had for him, but understanding his motives.

"I have a plan. I have a map." He stroked her cheek with the back of his hand. "I'm going to leave tomorrow and when I'm done walking I'll see you again. We'll spend time together and you'll know with 100% certainty that this is the real thing. No more frogs for Tiffany Bonander."

"I like the sound of that." She tried to smile, which was a useless gesture since he couldn't see her. "But could you stay a few more days, just to reassure me?"

"I can see how a few days would turn into months while you conducted your cocoa experiments." His voice wasn't entirely a refusal.

"At least sleep on it," she pressed.

She could feel his reluctance in his rigid muscles. "I have to do this, Tiff. Trust this little feeling, this little seed, and let it grow into something. Or tell me you don't feel the same and I'll ask Sister Mary Ofelia for a divorce in the morning."

And that was the problem. She did feel the same way. She'd never known a man so honest and genuine, so worthy of love. She felt as if she could tell him anything. And in turn, he wouldn't dismiss her aspirations, like Chad, or laugh at her footwear, like Adam. "What if I came with you?"

"We're on two different paths at the moment, Tiff. You need to cultivate your cocoa beans. I need to honor Owen."

"Why do you always have to be right?"

"Because I don't jump ahead. I live in the moment." He tucked her close against him. "Now, no more talking."

CHAPTER 9

JAX AWOKE in the gray light before dawn. Tiff slept on the cot next to him, her face relaxed in slumber.

She was determined save her family's company. She was equally determined he postpone his trip across Ecuador. She knew how dangerous Ecuador could be. She was worried something would go wrong—bugs, snakes, infection. He'd bet she'd stayed awake last night coming up with more arguments to make him stay and keep him safe.

He'd had a few himself last night, finally realizing that Owen should be the main motivator for his trek, not Jax's manhood. The longer he waited, the more likely he'd be to disappoint Owen and his family. In fact, there was an urgency to his leaving. Other men scarred by their military service would benefit from treks like this. He could organize them.

Suddenly, Jax knew what he had to do. He had to leave before Tiff woke up, before she came up with another batch of reasons he should stay, before he found merit in one of her arguments. He'd leave her with *unido* and the promise of a future between them.

It was Christmas morning. His sock liners above the hotplate should have dried completely. The river should have receded.

The bridge would be passable, even if he had to cross by walking on the girders. He could go. He had to go.

He drank in her beautiful face in case the connection they made fell apart. Or he died trying to do this.

You can stay.

He imagined returning to Phoenix without having crossed into the Andes. His father would say, "*I told you so.*" His mother would continue to treat him like an invalid.

He'd come here to do something that mattered. If his love for Tiff was meant to be, she'd wait for him. She was stronger than she gave herself credit for.

TIFF STRETCHED and opened her eyes to an empty bedroom. The convent was quiet. No creaking floorboards. No squeaky walkers. No shower. No... "*Jax?*"

She leapt to her feet and ran for her boots, bolting out the door without bothering to close it. She clumped down the stairs, down the path, nearly falling as she burst onto the road. "Jax!"

The road was empty.

Booted footprints in the mud headed downhill. There was no way to tell when he'd left or how far ahead of her he was.

She wanted another chance to talk him out of leaving. She wanted to say goodbye and feel the reassurance of his arms around her.

She ran in her pink boots and yoga pants, keeping to the middle of the road, trying not to lose her footing. Soon, the rapid gurgle of the river reached her.

One bend. Two. The road turned and widened down to the bridge.

The river had dropped enough that it barely covered the boards that were left. Crossing was still too dangerous.

Jax was making his way across, about five feet from the far side. His steps weren't sure. A board skittered against the low railing, nearly taking his prosthetic foot out from under him.

Twigs, branches, and unidentified things rushed around his ankles.

"*Jax!*"

He righted himself, reaching down to tug at his pants leg above his prosthetic. "Snake Bait."

She reminded herself to breathe, reminded herself she had no right to hold him here. In fact, it was better if he left. For him.

Jax carefully navigated the rest of the bridge and turned to face her. "Merry Christmas."

She wouldn't ask him to stay. Instead, she recorded every detail of his appearance in her memory. The endearingly crooked smile. The determined look in his blue eyes framed on one side by a purplish bruise. The stance that said nothing was going to stand in the way of his goals.

Except she was on his list of goals now. And he was leaving her behind.

She'd always done the leaving. Now she understood Chad's bitterness, Adam's lovesick stares, Malcolm's drunk dialing. She felt it all. The loneliness, the insignificance, the heartbreak.

Jax waited for her to say something. She could release him from *unido*. She should release him. But her heart rebelled at the idea, pounding as if it could work its way to Jax if it only beat fast enough.

Before she found her courage, he spoke. "About *unido*..."

Her heart sank into her pink boots. He was dumping her. Despite what he'd said last night. Why else would he sneak away without saying goodbye?

"I understand." She'd known what they had couldn't last. Karma was having the last word.

"About *unido*—"

"It's okay. It doesn't matter." What mattered was that he stayed safe. "Did you remember your gun?"

"Yes." He frowned. "You're okay with my leaving?"

She nodded when all she wanted to do was shake her head

and shout, "*No!*" She sucked all her panic into a tight ball in her belly. "What about the thunder? Promise me you won't go walking around in the rainforest during a thunderstorm."

"I took your bandana." Jax pulled the red square of cloth out of a side pocket in his cargo pants. "Your scent. It calms me. Together, we can beat this."

She was glad. She was oh-so-very glad he had a plan to stay safe. And if it didn't work, he'd figure something else out. She struggled to assemble a brave smile. "We'll always have Christmas. Our flooded, snake-infested, bug-filled, muggy Christmas." She swallowed back grief and soldiered a smile. "So this is goodbye."

"Tiff, you're jumping ahead." He scowled and propped his hands on his hips. "If you can do it, I can, too." He shook his head, as if in disapproval. "What was the name of that bed and breakfast your aunt runs in Cedar City? The one with the weddings?"

"The Iron Gate Inn?" What did that have to do with anything?

His frown turned into a determined look. "I'm going for a walk."

This is it. Tiff could barely nod. She certainly couldn't speak past the lump in her throat.

"Should take me a couple of months."

She nodded again. Being a bobblehead meant she felt no emotion, because the bobbing kept it all inside her. The hurt and disbelief snacked on her chest from the inside out.

"I'll meet you the last week in April at The Iron Gate Inn. That ought to give you enough time to develop your cocoa tree. I want you to email my friend, Gary." He rattled off a gmail address. "Tell him to get the boys together because at the end of our stay we're going to dissolve our *unido* agreement and get married. If you'll have me."

Tiff nearly slipped into the river.

"I'll show up. That's a promise. My father always told me a

Christmas promise couldn't be broken." He grinned. "You'll be there, right?"

She nodded, feeling as if she'd been side-swiped and left helpless on the side of the road. But of one thing, she was certain. Jax would rescue her.

"I promise we'll make this thing between us stronger than these old bridge girders." She could have sworn his gaze dropped to her lips, before reconnecting with her eyes. "I should have kissed you goodbye. I love you, wife."

He—

He was gone.

Before she could gather her wits.

Before she could say he was a fool.

And that she loved him, too.

Curious about the next book in the series?
Always a Bridesmaid, **Book 2 in The Bridesmaid Series**

୧୨୬

Part of an Email from Jackson (the groom) to Tiffany (the bride):
Tiff, I'm here in the Andes staring at the stars. They seem closer than you
are, Snake Bait, even though I know you're closer, because you're right
here in my heart. Can't wait until April. Love, Jax

CHAPTER 1

There was going to be a wedding in two months between
Jackson Hardaway and Tiffany Bonander.

If the bride didn't run away with the caterer.

Or the wedding planner.

Or someone equally as interesting and attractive. If she didn't
simply decide she didn't love the man enough.

That's what Tiff had done to her five previous fiancés – broke
things off. With five someones. *Five!* All thrown back in New
York City's dating pool. This wedding was for Catch No. 6.

Master baker Nicole Edwards couldn't catch one man, much
less half a dozen. Nicole wanted to tell Tiff there was a time to
fish, and a time to cut bait. If Catch No. 6 didn't work out, give
the other girls in New York City a chance to reel one in.

In the time it took Tiff to nab all those fiancés, Nicole had
been a bridesmaid thirteen times.

Thirteen times! If that wasn't enough to put a woman's biological clock in a panic, Nicole didn't know what was.

"Thirteen is a sign, my angel," Grandma Redhair had said to Nicole
in her thick Russian accent on New Year's Day. "The number one symbol-
izes you. Alone. For the rest of your life." Grandma Redhair had shaken
her purple prayer rope so vehemently that the scarf covering the thin
strands of red hair left on her head had slid to her crown. "And the

number three symbolizes the life balance you have achieved, the balance that has led you to love's dead end. You have the Siberian Curse."

"Babushka," Nicole's mother had chastised from the kitchen. "Don't fill Nicole's head with nonsense. There is no Siberian Curse."

According to Grandma Redhair, the Siberian Curse caused women to freeze up at the sight of a desirable man and become invisible. It was real, all right. And Nicole had it. Put an intelligent, good-looking man in front of her, and Nicole became as animated as the Statue of Liberty.

"I tell her the truth." Grandma Redhair spat – right there on Mom's Oriental rug! "And wish for her luck to change. But will it? No! Because Nicole balances her joy of baking in one hand and her drive for success in the other. Where is the hand to hold love? This is why she freezes. She holds too much. She has to give up something to get something and break the curse."

Grandma Redhair's words had stuck with Nicole through a cold and snowy January, making her look at her life with a critical eye. She had employees to work the bakery counter, a liaison to deal with wedding coordinators, and an assistant baker. On the one hand, all Nicole had to do was bake in the bakery's basement. On the other hand, all Nicole did was bake in the bakery's basement. There wasn't much time built in to do much more than be a bridesmaid.

Grandma Redhair was right. Her love life had dead ended. She had two choices: give up on love (and babies) or give up on baking (and happiness). Nicole had walked around indecisively with her biological timepiece for weeks.

And then Nicole saw an online article about the top ten places to eat on a date. Among the listings? Food trucks, including dessert-themed ones. A link at the bottom of the article led to statistics on towns with higher ratios of single men to single women. And there sat Los Angeles, one of the food truck capitols of the nation. Call it karma. Call it fate. An idea took shape.

Since her best baking decisions were spur-of-the-moment, Nicole immediately put her bakery up for sale and made plans to relocate to L.A. and buy a food truck. She'd beat the Siberian Curse. How could she not? She'd be a one person show – forced to interact with the public, including attractive men. So what if the thought gave her hives. Moving to L.A. would be like being dumped in the middle of the Hudson River – swim or perish. Not that she was completely fearless. She'd wait until she moved to L.A. to test her theory.

And so she gratefully gave up her Valentine's weekend to work. Bon-Bon Chocolate heiress, Tiffany Bonander (one of Nicole's best clients) planned to take her latest wedding to Catch No. 6 on the road to her aunt's beautiful bed & breakfast – The Iron Gate Inn in Cedar City, Utah. That's where Tiff's wedding planner, caterer, baker (a.k.a., Nicole), and future in-laws were spending Valentine's weekend – doing a run-through of potential menus for April's destination wedding. Other guests at The Iron Gate Inn were being treated to the same gourmet dinner and dessert menus as the wedding party.

Nicole paused in the back entry to the inn's gourmet kitchen. Chef Sean O'Malley, the wedding caterer, had his white jacket sleeves rolled up, and was dicing carrots. His cooking form was a thing of beauty. His face and physique weren't bad either.

Sean glanced up at her with those intense green eyes, the ones that could pierce you for making a culinary mistake. He'd been dubbed their generation's version of the prickly Gordon Ramsey, while Nicole was generally likened to the friendly Cake Boss. Sean was all about barked orders and rigid schedules. Nicole was more the soft-spoken wishes and impromptu decisions type of gal. But somehow their dishes were wonderful together, which meant they often worked the same events.

Sean was tall and broad shouldered, with thick, red-brown hair that curled stubbornly over his forehead. That was the thing Nicole loved best about his appearance. That curl said Sean wasn't perfect. She reasoned that his imperfect curl, along with his Chef High & Mighty attitude, blocked the Siberian Curse, because she never froze when he was around.

"You're late," Sean grumbled. "You should be prepping your dessert."

"I have plenty of extra time." Words tripped easily off her tongue. "Recall that I don't work for you, Chef. As a courtesy, I sent you a text message when I left Vegas." The closest major airport, a good three hours away.

Sean made a derogatory sound, and reached for a clove of garlic. His movements were culinary poetry, contained power and crisp execution.

What woman wouldn't experience a heart-stopping *ka-thunk* while watching him? Nicole had a fantasy about Sean involving his ability to slice and dice. Flowers, that is. She imagined him visiting a garden, divesting it of blooms, and spreading them over a bed around her. It was a foolish notion given it was about Chef High & Mighty, but it was one she'd been unable to shake.

When Tiff became engaged the first time, Nicole had only known Sean by reputation. She'd agreed to meet Tiff at the reception hall to check out the refrigeration units and there he was – gorgeous and smart, but gruff and grumpy – the antidote to the Siberian Curse. They'd argued over the appropriateness of the kitchen. As a master baker, Nicole had specific requirements that Sean didn't share. She preferred equipment that was top of the line, not new and untested, but not too old either.

Her gaze drifted to Sean, noting the subtle lines that fanned out from his eyes. She'd never noticed those lines before. They didn't make him look old. They made him seem...less Chef High & Mighty and more human.

Human? Must be a trick of the light. Nicole blinked and moved past him to the sink.

Garlic pressed, Sean reached for a sweet potato. He cut it with the quick, steady cadence of a marching band's drummer. "Your text was a little...vague."

"Vague?" Nicole washed her hands. The window over the sink offered a view of the Iron Gate Inn's planked back porch, parking lot, and small winery. All were covered with three feet of softly sloping fresh snow. "I said I was leaving Vegas."

The percussion session ended. Sean didn't look up. His knife paused mid-air. "Do you have a new phone?"

"Yeah. How did you know?" She'd gotten a new phone just yesterday and was still in the love-hate phase, discovering – *or not* – how things worked.

"Check the message you sent me." That holier-than-thou tone of his always hit her wrong, as if someone had put dough in a food processor on puree when it should have been hand-folded.

Nicole pulled out her phone, toggled to his message and read, "*Doodles, I'm live in Vegas now. Are you making porn tonight?*" She raised her phone to heaven, feeling her cheeks heat. She bet Chef High & Mighty never texted with typos. "Dang auto correct. I swear, I typed in: *Dude, I'm leaving Vegas now. Are you making pork tonight?*" Pork chops was one of his signature dishes. Meat was his specialty. Being inspired by a chef's menu to create a unique dessert was hers.

The chopping resumed. "I thought you'd given up baking and were asking me to join you in an illicit venture."

Was that a smile teasing the corner of his mouth?

Something whisked through her chest with breath-stealing intensity, like the winds from the mountains in Siberia. She searched Sean's face. But whatever expression he'd made, it disappeared as quickly as it'd come, allowing her to breathe again.

Silence descended upon the kitchen, and with it came a rare moment of reflection. Nicole had a free hour before she had to make her dessert. The gentle creak of the old inn, Sean's dinner prep minus his usual shouted commands, the absence of traffic noise. It was quiet. It was peaceful. It was all wrong.

She had no pressing to-do list. No employees lining up with questions. No clock ticking down while she willed time to slow.

Was this what her life would be like in L.A.? *Downtime? Free time? Boredom?*

She suppressed a shiver. Inertia was her curse. If she didn't have enough to do in L.A., she'd start to over-eat again. Even now, her gaze darted around the room looking for chocolate. Oh, yeah. Without fourteen hour days, she'd gain weight in the City of Angels. Instead of turning guys on, she'd once more become the fat butt of their jokes. It'd be middle school all over again.

Her pulse throbbed in her temple.

Choose love. Free a hand.

If she freed a hand, she'd reach for a Twinkie. She'd eat a pan of cheesecake brownies, a baker's dozen of Snickerdoodles, éclair filling straight from the pastry tube.

Her fingers cramped around her cell phone. Listing the business for sale was a huge mistake.

If only she had a recipe to dispel the Siberian Curse. She could stay in New York. She could hire another baker. She'd go out at night and say intelligent things when an attractive man was near. She'd fall in love, get married, have babies, and never have to be a bridesmaid again.

There had to be a recipe to break the curse. She'd pay anything for it.

Her gaze landed on a distraction – Sean's undressed vegetables. They sat in a baking dish on the island, like a poor man's offering to the dinner gods. So plain. They pleaded with her for life, for an ingredient or two to save them – brown sugar, pumpkin spice, lemon peel, anything. They'd settle for a lonely sprig of rosemary.

How pathetic that she could think of ingredients to improve Sean's plain veggies, but she couldn't come up with a recipe for love.

Get a grip. She did have a recipe. One of her own making: *Sell the bakery and move to L.A.* Baking in a food truck she could work as much or as little as she wanted. More when she was single. Less when she found that special someone.

Nicole relaxed her grip on her cell phone, and said the words she hadn't uttered to anyone. "This is my last wedding." After Tiff's celebration in two months, the next wedding cake Nicole made would be her own.

Sean didn't just stop chopping this time. He set the knife down and turned a sharp gaze on her. "Say again."

She wasn't sure she could say it again. She had to swallow twice to dredge up the words. "I listed my bakery for sale and I'm moving to L.A." There. She'd told someone she knew. That made it more real than signing the contract with the realtor.

"There's no foot traffic in L.A. Your morning sales will tank."

Thank you, Mr. Sunshine.

"And your catering business..." His gaze cornered her insecurities and spotlighted her shaky resolve. "You'll struggle to find bookings. Who will you bake for?"

Nicole clenched her jaw. "I'm giving up catering. I'm going to buy a food truck and be plenty busy." She set the oven to preheat. May as well bake cookies for the guests while she was in the kitchen.

Sean looked as if he'd swallowed a pepperoncini, one that stuck in his throat. "You can't leave New York for a food truck."

"I can. I am. Nobody's going to stop me." Nobody seemed to want to try.

Want to read more?

Grab your copy of *Always a Bridesmaid* today!

THANK YOU!

Thank you for reading this installment of The Bridesmaids sweet novella series by Melinda Curtis. The next installments in the series feature Tiffany and her bridesmaids as they prepare for the Bon-Bon Bride's wedding and fall in love.

Book 1: The Wedding Promise

Book 2: Always a Bridesmaid

Book 3: Rescued by a Bridesmaid

Book 4: You May Now Kiss the Bridesmaid

Book 5: The Bridesmaid Wore White

Read about Tiffany's cousins in The Kissing Test series. Look for the first book *A Kiss is Just a Kiss* – out now!

Would you like to know when Melinda's next book is coming out? Sign up for her book release email list at www.MelindaCurtis.com (in return you'll receive a free read), or like her Facebook page at https://www. facebook.com/MelindaCurtisAuthor.

If reviewing is your thing, thank you. Reviews help readers find books.

Look for other sweet romances from Melinda Curtis published by Harlequin Heartwarming, Forever Romance, and Caezik Romance.

What other authors are saying about Melinda's Books...

Jayne Ann Krentz says of *Can't Hurry Love:* "Nobody does emotional, heartwarming small-town romance like Melinda Curtis. This is a wonderful tonic of a book."

Brenda Novak says of *Season of Change:* "Reading Slade and Christine's story reminded me of why I enjoy romance. SEASON OF CHANGE has found a place on my keeper shelf!"

ACKNOWLEDGMENTS

Many of Tiffany's jungle experiences are based on the travels of my dear friend, Kim Wilson, who founded Good King Organic Cacao, which provides women around the globe income opportunities. Visit their website to learn more and support this important effort by buying their chocolate. I couldn't have finished this novella without the love and support of my family and friends. As always, Mr. Curtis was patient during the completion of this project (being smart enough to accept a new job so he'd be busy working while I put in additional hours). My undying thanks to my writing group – Anna J. Stewart and Cari Lynn Webb. And thank you, dear reader, for reading.

Made in the USA
Monee, IL
20 June 2023

36286299R00050